MEMORY AND BRAIN SCIENCE

The 4th Dimension of Learning

Dr. Vinod Sharma

First Published in April 2022

ISBN: 978-93-5611-323-7

BLUEROSE PUBLISHERS

www.BlueRoseONE.com

info@bluerosepublishers.com

+91 8882 898 898

Cover Design:

Aveek

Typographic Design:

Rohit

Distributed by: BlueRose, Amazon, Flipkart

PROFILE OF AUTHOR
DR. VINOD SHARMA

- Guinness World Record holder.
- Internationally awarded and renowned as memory expert.
- Many of his programs have been telecasted on national TV channels and radio.
- Has served companies like NIS, Sparta, Future group and Max India as a corporate trainer with more than 6 years of experience.
- Has addressed more than 10 lakh trainees so far.
- Brain science article/ story writer.
- Shiksha Shastri .
- Working in the field of brain science and its development for the last 10 years.
- Holds national record in mimicry of imitating 256 voices .
- Highly acclaimed motivational speaker .
- Set three world records in one day including Asia Book of Records, India Book of Records and Guinness World Records .
- Best memory and mnemonic trainer award in 2016.
- Record of decade in India Book of Record 2016 .
- A renowned writer and columnist , his column MIND IT has been a well acclaimed regular weekly article in Rajasthan Partrika. Many of his writings have been published as cover stories in leading newspapers
- Many of his students have created National Records
- Awarded for being chosen in Top 100 record holders at world stage.
- Awarded with honorary doctorate in brain science field by World Record University , UK

PREFACE

Hello everyone, Welcome to the World of learning. But let me tell you one thing , one day, I had quarrel with my Dad , my Dad is a very angry man . this morning also he was fighting over a topic , I told him , I've always seen you frustrated , annoyed and always in a ruthless mood, was there any day or any moment in you life when you were happy ? My Dad told me – " Oh yes there was only one day when I was actually very happy in life"; very curiously I asked him what happened that day ? To which he answered that I got the highest percentage of my life that day and that day was when my 10th board results were out . I again questioned him how much percentage he scored? He answered – 55%. I laughed to my core when I heard this and might be possible that most of you also are laughing after reading this . I questioned him that tell me one thing – when you scored 55% everyone around you was happy and celebrating and distributing sweets and when I scored 65% in my academics , you went angry and started beating me ! Why you being so biased ? I scored much better then you at least. To this my dad told me that my son when I scored 55% then in the whole school, society, community I scored the highest of all, but when you scored 65% then among many people in the school, community and society, your grades were not up to the mark. Then at that moment I understood that getting good grades and percentage Is not important , but what is more important is that at that particular time how many people score that percentage , and this called as MSV- Mark Sheet Value. During my Father's time MSV was 55% and during my school time MSV was 75% and now it is raised upto 95%. Every parent now a days want that his/her child should score good that is 95% ,and might be even possible that the one who is reading this book currently also want the same , which means that today MSV value is more than 90%. Now it is clearly understood that scoring 95% requires more efforts and more time then scoring 55% and that is why if look at the schedule of today's student – he spend 8 hours in school, coaching institute 1 hour, then school home work 1 hour , he gives 1 hour to revise school work and 1-2 hour to revise whatever is being taught at coaching institute, put together these are 15 hours minimum If he wants to score 95% . This means that 15 hours he requires for studying and 8 hours of sleep, therefore which means that around he spends 23 hours like this and how many hours are actually in the day ....24 hours! Out of which 23 hours are already gone in just scoring these 95% and now in that remaining 1 hour the child has to do all the basic necessities i.e bathing , eating food, roaming here and there , going out on vacation , meeting friends or working on the any of his hobbies or if the parents wants his child to learn about the society , culture , community or if any other skill apart from academics which needs to be develop .....So for all these things how much time is left with the child only 1 hour!! Then can any one of these qualities be developed ? ....NO!! now the thing is that the maximum time we spent on studies how much important is that in life? Now let me ask one question to the reader that you might know there are many of people who are not that much qualified in academics but still doing very well in life and are highly successful ..... Dhirubhai Ambani, Amitabh Bacchan, Sachin Tendulkar (who failed in 10th class), but you might know many of the people in your families and surroundings , near dear friends, relatives who are also not that qualified but who has a lot of name and fame and these people are highly qualified. And ironically in India 95% of the top class Businessmen are not well qualified in academics but doing very well in their field. That means the opposite of this as in the people are well qualified in the academics or are gold medalist in their subjects but still are unsuccessful and aren't getting the desired success and are still struggling with a compromised and frustrated job. 99% of the youth in India faces the same. The child is getting good score but he isn't getting the success with those particular grades. Now the question arises that what is 100% success?

Success is this Pyramid.

HOLISTIC SUCCESS PYRAMID

To build a pyramid we require more space at the bottom , pyramids are consider to be most strengthen structure , they aren't even affected by the any earthquake . just because of the structure i.e broader at the bottom and narrower at the top , the pyramids are the most balanced structure and it can never be destroyed. The child should inherit the same type of strength . The question now arises that how is it possible? It is possible if the child start doing his studies in the similar pyramid shape too. Let me get into more detail of this pyramid – if you look at the pyramid closely you will notice that where pyramid is more broader that skill requires more attention in a child's life which means that in this pyramid the important skill starts from bottom to top i.e the skill mentioned at the bottom of the pyramid is most important as compared to the top one, the top one is also important but not more the bottom one. The most important is the "Behavioral Skill Development", the least important is "academic and mark sheet development" and what I think and concluded (from the above example also) even if you remove the top most part of the pyramid then also you can succeed in your life. But in India , when I told that the pyramid is important from bottom to up, parents flipped this pyramid i.e

Parents in the present day gives importance to academic and mark sheet and the least importance is given to the other skills and the child grows this with skill only. Now again the question arises that after so many efforts still why the people are not successful , the reason being fundamental mistake . let me now explain what is fundamental mistake- as we all know a car has 4 wheels and one the wheel is punctured and if you do not repair that one wheels and keeps on driving with that punctured wheel , will your reach to the destination? Answer is No. if the wheel is punctured we have three options- 1. Manage with that puncture wheel and don't use that car , 2. Get that wheel repaired ,3. Fill in with air that wheel for a particular time period and then after again repeat the same. Which is best option among the three? Yes you guessed it correct i.e the that wheel repaired.

Now let me tell you something more interesting , your education is a car and has four wheels , among the four one of the wheel is punctured and till date is not repaired – these four wheels can be defined as cognigence, kinesthetic, comprehension and recollection or in a layman term is can be called as reading for which we have coursebooks, writing for which we have notebooks, understanding for which we have our school teachers and recollection. Since childhood we've been taught how to read, write and understand and there fore we do not face any problem in these three but let's talk about recollection ....we've never been trained on recollection and hence we always face problems in recollecting subjects. The important all the four wheels is recollection. In India , exams holds such an important part in an education system and what is exam ? exam is itself is a recollection skill. Exam is the time to recollect.

You read newspapers , do you recollect? Because there is not need of recollection of newspaper, moreover there is no exam of newspaper. But during the time when the child studies he always asked that you need to recollect this and this will be asked in exam . therefore the 4th dimension of education is science of recollection. With accurate recollection the child will score more and if there is a mistake or poor recollection it will affect the exam result accordingly. Therefore this wheel of education has become the most important of all . if you to market to buy a shirt for yourself and you have two options-the one which has less durability costing Rs 400/- and another which has a good quality and longer shelf life costing Rs 600/-, among them which shirt you want to purchase? Maximum number of people will choose the 2nd option which has more durability. Which means we invest time and money where we see the durability and permanency , which it is such a big fault that have not done the same with a child's education . everyone one of us is just concerned with what a child is studying and how much grades he will score in the exam but none of us is concerned till how long that knowledge can be recollected and holds a permanent place in our mind. Actually no one is concerned that after exam how long that knowledge can still be recollected . if you ask your teacher that how shall I study so that I am able to recollect things till my lifetime , the teacher has no answer to this . you being a parent , a teacher , don't you think that permanent recollection is important ? this is the reason why child is not able use that knowledge in his lifetime. Why are studying ? just to memorize that subject ? that knowledge provides some or the other development in our life , but that development will only takes place only when it is a permanent knowledge . if you to gym for 2 days or 1 full day in a month , it won't make a difference , until and unless you won't make this as a permanent habit or make it a part of your lifestyle you won't see any results. Similarly the knowledge which a child gets through his studies also needs to be permanent . if you have an ATM card and you remember the pin of your card can you use that card for withdrawing money? Answer is NO. similarly when a child completes his studies he forgets 99% of what he has studied. This is the reason when the child reaches to the peak time , he struggles because nor he has skills as he didn't worked on it , neither he remember the knowledge which he studied and then again to be successful he reaches out to some other lines and again his struggles starts. That is why even after formal education the child undergo many types of other education also to build his career e.g MBA, MCA …etc. to all these problem there is only one solution that is we build a strong base to our education that is we start working on making our knowledge permanent .Therefore recollection is important and the science of recollection is only known as brain science , which is the fourth dimension of education . Even in the official library of UNESCO there is the book by Daniel Richard on the science of recollection. Mnemonic science supports this recollection science. Mnemonic science means to memorize any effectively and interestingly . if we use mnemonic science in studies , it will result in –

1. Better exam results
2. Fast memorization
3. Permanent memory which results in accurate recollection
4. Reduce the time by 70%

Everywhere around us , there is a stressed environment in terms of education , and when the exams are nearby the phobia starts moreover there are lot many cases of suicides coming out just because of the stress and depression caused by the education ; this is happening because the one wheel of education is missing that is recollection . You will notice that all the students commit suicide after the result and not during the studies. In our education system this recollection is missing , recollection is on demand but the training for recollection missing . this book will provide you training on recollection and memory training .

Now the question arises that how to understand this book . Let us first understand the word Brain Science Training , Training converts the knowledge into skills , We are scared to see a lion is in jungle but we enjoy to see that same lion in circus , a trainer changed the behavioral skill of that wild animal. When a wild animal can be trained then don't you think that even a child requires this sort of training in his life? So this book will give you training over knowledge .

Next lets understand the word Science – by which human effort and human time is reduced in fast and effective way. E.g - if will be want to travel and cover the distance of 100 kms and if to walk and cover the same you will require 2 days but by car you can cover the same 2 hours , by this example you can understand what is the meaning of science . in early ages , people write letters and now a days they take the help of whatsapp , this is also possible with the help of science .Science does 3 things in your life – reduces time, reduces effort, and increases comfort. But lets talk about our studies ,in last 30 years the time has only increased, which clearly indicates that we study science but we don't use science in studies . In our life how science reduces the human effort and human time in the same way Brain Science reduces the learning time and learning effort and this book all about this. In this book you learn some the methods , in this book will also learning the balancing of both right and left brain and you will also learn how to be creative . you will learn how to be creatively logical . Our human brain has an inbuilt and most unique quality known as creativity . some people are logical and some are creative , the ones who are logical they take least interest in creative work e.g principal, politician , mathematician , rationalist and on the other hand the ones who are creative e.g musician, painter, artists , if you give them logical work they won't take interest in doing the same . but some fall in a category of being both that is the people who are creatively logical known as scientist that is they create, they imagine first in their brain and they come out to the conclusion with the logic that how it can be made.

Einstein once said that the children who fall in the age group of 9 years to 16 years in the world , they have a similar brain pattern to that of a scientist that means they are creatively logical . this science will make you learn how to be creatively logical in education.

Therefore I hope that after reading this book , and once you thoroughly understand this book , in some part of your logical studies along with some geography, economy, polity, science, definition, derivation, vocabulary , dictionary , diagrams, long answer, short answer , you'll be able to memorize and recollect such kind of things on a faster pace and very efficiently and quickly.

So, lets start with the book , you have to read the chapters as they are given and try to apply that method in your studies . I am sure you will enjoy your studies with the help of Brain Science.

If you face any kind of problem or have any kind of questions or quires regarding any topic you can directly contact us on 7665500321 or on www.vinodsharma.co.in.

Yours,

Vinod Sharma

Mail – vinodsharmabrainscience@gmail.com

CONTENTS

BRAINYWOOD

Inspiration

BRAINYWOOD- A NOBLE MISSION IN EDUCATION

A project started with a vision to "Reform and empower education system to make learning process complete with the help of **4th dimension of education**– Science of Recollection and reducing the education expenses of parents, reducing the study time, removing the study stress of students and making every child intelligent to make children asset to the nation eventually. Giving scientific approach in studies and making education meaningful for students."

Brainywood is an ed-tech learning application that focuses on providing complete education solutions in one place to all the students of our nation at the very most affordable prices. The academic courses and all other training programs on Brainywood application are based on educational psychology to give psychological solutions to students to enjoy their studies and exams. Students usually forget the content even after memorizing so many times. Brainywood unique feature is that it deals with removing the habit of forgetting by converting the study content into permanent memory with the help of imagination and association. Brainywood gives student's new and proven techniques of mnemonic science based on educational psychology, especially skilling students on memorization retention and recollection. By which students, enjoy the syllabus, memorize faster and recollect the content exams accurately. Brainywood helps students in converting the study content into visuals to memorize fast and helps to reduce the study time. We use the **theory of imagination** and **association** which enables students to make study interesting, increasing concentration, learning effectively, and most importantly it gives permanent memory for students so students do not forget the content not only till exams but till so long in life.

Brainywood completes the education learning cycle – Reading, writing, understanding, memorization, retention, and finally Recollection.

Project Brainywood was started back in 2015, by Dr. Vinod Sharma (Founder) and Mr. Dhruv Suwalka (Co-Founder) is now having a team of 100+ (that comprises India's best teachers, counselors, educationists, brain science experts, and trainers), 1000+ Franchisees working across India, including some working in Saudi Arabia, USA, Dubai, Bangladesh, Nepal that collectively impacted the lives of over 1 lakh+ student and counting.

The entire team of Brainywood believes that Quality education should be right for all, not their privilege.

Finally, I dedicate this book to my parents, my son Ayaan and my wife Megha.

I am thankful to all my family, mentors, and team members for inspiring me always.

Yours,

Vinod Sharma

You can reach out to me at vinodsharmabrainscience@gmail.com or by visiting the following websites.

https://brainywoodindia.com/

https://vinodsharma.co.in/

THE MISSION

What is the purpose of formal education? The purpose is to develop a mark sheet or to develop intelligence?

How can we reduce the study time, study stress and study expenses without tempering the desired result?

How to serve quality education to 350 million middle-class family's children at a very low cost?

What we want our children to be – successful or meritorious? If we do have only one choice, most people will go with the 1st choice i.e. successful. Today students are being educated or studying because we think good education is important for success, but do we agree there so many people who are not so educated formally and yet highly successful and the reverse is just as true, there are so many people who are highly educated formally and yet struggling hard for desired success, so getting good marks and being formally educated is just the stepping stone towards success but it's not the holistic success. So what is the Holistic success? Success is something that is directly related to the brain. We eat food to survive and grow our body similarly our brain has food which is called knowledge and skill. Education has so many pieces of knowledge but what about the skills which must come through education and those skills must be founded upon basic education. Skills are very important because knowledge is always appreciated but in a practical world, skills are rewarded.

We at BRAINYWOOD believes the 'purpose of education', is all about translating knowledge into skills. There are two things one is a body and the other is a soul and we agree with the saying that "results will come when the body with soul is in action". Importantly actions must be coupled with values which means "doing the right thing for the right reason". Understand this phase in a way that the teachers are teaching and the students are being educated, which means teachers are doing the right thing, but what is the reason for teaching or studying? Marks or skills? The present scenario says that marks are being emphasized but skills are overlooked because most students do not know what skills will be developed by the subjects they are studying. A surprising fact is that the students study hard and get good marks but after some time they forget most of the things, this shows that our education system is doing the right thing for the wrong reason. For instance, why do we learn driving? So as to have a driving license or to actually learn driving. We all learn driving because we want to learn how to drive, driving is a skill which we actually want to have it but a driving license is a symbol of that particular skill in your pocket and that is needed because of the administrative formality. Suppose govt. stops distributing license will we stop learning driving? No, which means the license is the requirement by the government; my requirement is just to learn driving. Similarly why we are studying? For the mark sheet or because we want to study that would make us inculcate some kind of skills or some kind of development in our life. So we must be doing the right thing for the right reason. License is the symbol, we should have a license, alike driving license mark sheets is just the symbol of our knowledge and skills. So doing the right thing for the right reason transpires that in education there must be good teaching, good education, good study not because we want to score marks but to get the learning for life, for success and for holistic development.

In our surroundings what has actually developed or improvised in the past years or which keeps on improvising day by day is **"science"**. We call development is taking place in a nation when the "science" is actually improvising or developed, and the development of science is directly proportionate to the development of life, development of society, development of the entire ecosystem.

If we would look closely we will find out the computers, communication, machines, business processes have improved dramatically since midcentury but Indian education has remained the same for years.

Modern Phone Today

hone 100 years back

Modern Car Today

Car 100 years back

Modern Classroom Today

Classroom 100 years back

In 100 years time what has been improvised in our Indian education system is only the body of the education, the hardware of the education like the classrooms, the smart boards, the internet facilities, computers, etc. These all are important for every nation's education system but the problem is only the body of education is being improvised, what about the soul i.e. skill, knowledge? Our body is being developed but our soul (body) is standing still. The purpose of education is to turn knowledge into skill and in order to turn knowledge into skill, there is the process called a learning cycle. Brain science helps to complete the learning cycle before we understand the brain science, we need to understand the importance of science first.

The development of science manages to reduce the time, efforts and increase the comfortability for people. For instance, if we cover 100 km by foot (walking) it will take us around 2-3 days and it will be a tiring job to do but if we cover the same distance by car then it would take only 2-3 hours with comfort. This shows that we can significantly reduce the time, efforts and increase the comfortability with the help of science. As science reduces human time and effort likewise the brain science reduces the learning time and effort and increases comfortability in studying.

Our Knowledge is scattered in the brain but it needs to be channelized. This can be done through brain science.

Further, the science also reduces stress, covering 100 km via feet was big stress but covering it by car or helicopter is not a stress, which means as much you are scientific in approach your stress gets reduced. If we talk about education, education is being developed, along with the education development, stress is increasing or decreasing? Of course, increasing. So why it is so?

Science is meant to reduce the time, effort and stress but in context to students the time and stress are increasing because "we are burning house for killing a mosquito". We are doing the right thing for the wrong reasons. It's more like we study science but we don't apply science in studies.

Today nobody is talking about skills but everybody is talking about marks. Parents, teachers, education system are centralized towards marks and that's why there are so many coaching institutes. We actually know what to do but we are overlooking how to do

Science does not say that students should not score good marks but for that his skills must be developed, his learning time, efforts and stress should reduce not increase day by day. Brain science gives students the right reason for the right actionable, which would give a good result, reduce study time and eventually give the multiple quotients and finally skills development.

The purpose of education is even to make people successful on time. Success on time is important, only success is not important. Suppose you get successful at the age of 99 years but that success is absolutely good for nothing but if you are successful on time like 26 or 30 years then you can enjoy your life and you can actually give a meaning to your life. Today our Indian students are living life meaningless because somewhere our Indian education is meaningless since students spent the most time on education and with teachers, we at Brainywood believes that the purpose of education is to make the students the assets to the nation. Do you think that all the students or all the citizens around the nation are assets? Ironically most of the students are considered as a liability. Most of them become those strugglers who do not have any purpose or direction in life.

There is a very old saying that "direction importation for the situation" right direction leads to the right situation and the wrong direction leads to the wrong situation. So the wrong situation is something in which most today students are into because now a day's students are directionless, they don't know where to go. Vivekananda Ji used to say after having the knowledge, what is next? This means if you are a student and having the knowledge then you should know what is next in life and what is best in your life but today the ironical situation is that even after completing education the students ask what to do in life? They don't know where to be directed. So education has a loophole here and in this report, you will find out what are these loopholes and why the problems are occurring, there's a scientific reason behind it.

Now not only the students are suffering but the parents are suffering at the same pace because students have a tremendous load of studies on them and simultaneously parents have a tremendous load of expenses. India is a country where you can have a loan for all most everything – you want to purchase gold, you have a gold loan, you want to purchase a house then you have a house loan, you can avail car loan if you want to purchase a car, but these all are the likings. Similarly in India, we also have an education loan. Sadly in our nation, for a good education, we need to take loans. How sarcastic is this? That means education is the basic needs and if the parent wants to have this basic need for their children they need to take the loan also. Hypothetically, this means after sometimes for clothing and eating also we might need to take some kind of loan. Our belief is that basic education is everybody's right not their privilege. Why do we need to take loans for the basic education of our children?

Why the coaching industry is actually hovering around? Because of the marks. Students want good marks and parents want to see their child scoring good marks. Schools and coaching institutes are teaching children about what is important to score marks but how to score good marks with less effort and time is no one teaching. For self-studies the students are helpless and that's why the coaching centres come in. The coaching industry is not only devouring the hard-earned money of Indian parents but also sucking out the important time of life of students. So these are the problem we all must be agreeing upon and it should be resolved in order to bring reform in our Indian education system.

In this project report, there are so much factual data and analysis involved where you will find students are committing suicide in the state of depression. Education is a state of expression but education fetching depression, why? There are so many students which could have been an asset to the nation but now they are no more, why? So why it happened?

It happened because of the negligence towards the learning cycle or not knowing the education psychology so far. It is well said and well defined in the education of psychology and sarcastically if any person who wants to do B. Ed – Bachelor of Education has to undergo two subjects those are – education psychology and education philosophy.

So if a teacher is reading and studying about education psychology during his B.ED, then why aren't they are using the same to teach the students? Brain science is already a part of education in B. Ed but unfortunately, it's been completely overlooked till yet in the schooling education system. We rephrased the education cycle and emphasizing the 4th dimension of education that is the science of recollection. Suppose you are in 9th or 10th class and you have your exams in 2-3 hours and you have around 120-150 question and answers, then what will you do – I have two ways, one is the traditional way that would take a long time and the chances of forgetting are very high and there I have got a new innovative method which is actually not new but not known, which is called as brain science method. With the help of these methods, 120-150 questions can be prepared and learned easily and you can get your desired marks by saving your time up to 70%. Moreover, these methods not just help you to achieve your desired marks but also enhance your skills and make you a skilled personality with the help of that knowledge. So this is brain science all about. Our start-up is based on brain science and actually, it is very burning need of current scenario and phenomena where the students are in stress, the expense of parents are surprising and the teachers are not knowing where and what to teach to students.

PROBLEM STATEMENT

The technology or the smart phones that distinct us from our surroundings also distinct us from the fact that our surroundings are strangely old in some aspects which have been overlooked till yet. Even today the teacher talks endlessly and dictatorially and the student listen passively and submissively which has discouraged questioning, discovery, experimentation, and application in the school classroom.

We teach every young student the same subjects in mostly the same ways, irrespective of individual talents, preferences and one pace. Imagine if a doctor gives the same prescribed medicine for all of its patients then the result of this would be terrible and this is what actually happening with today's students in India.

In the end, we are only concerned about how much a child is scoring. Students who not able to learn best by sitting still at the desk are made to feel somehow inferior and insecure, and the one with the highest grade receives status and credentials. Today grades are being considered as the precise measurement for student competitiveness but none of us is concerned about till how long that knowledge can be recollected and holds a permanent place in our mind. Actually, no one concerned that after the exam how long that knowledge can still be recollected. Moreover parents are spending heavy expenses in a child's education. Child isn't able to develop any of the skill, due to non scientific approach which ultimately leads to stress.

Children join the school as a question mark; they leave school with the same question mark?

Today students find studies uninteresting. "Why am I learning what I am learning?" and, "I don't remember anything I learned in school" are the common questions of most of the students nowadays. Due to a lack of innovation and scientific approach in studies today boredom, lack of involvement, time-consuming, stress, and suicidal attempts are the unfortunate results of today's education.

According to the **2012-Lancet Report**, India registered one of the highest suicide rates among youths in the world, who are between 15 and 29 years of age clearing pointing at increasing depression in Indian youth. The report mentions that the depression rate in India is rising alarmingly.

Earlier this year, **Hansraj Ahir**, the **Indian Minister of State for Home Affairs** stated in the **Lok Sabha** that about 9,474 students committed suicide only in the year 2016. This translates to about 26 suicides per day.

	Year 2014	Year 2015	Year 2016	Year 2007-16
No. of Students Suicides	8934	8068	9474	75000

Why Narendra Modi is concerned about depression among students in India

3 min read . Updated: 01 Aug 2017, 04:52 PM IST

Sanjay Kumar, Pranav Gupta

A student commits suicide in India every hour; how can our educational system prevent this?

Society, parents, educational system need to join hands for the holistic well-being of children

[illegible]

Save

In India, One Student Commits Suicide Every 55 Minutes. Yet, Depression Is Conveniently Ignored

IN DEPTH

[World Mental Health Day] India has the highest number of suicides among youth. So, what ails our young girls?

The Biggest Problem On Indian Campuses Is A Hidden One: Depression.

As per the report conducted on Indian Secondary school, it is distressing to note that around **6%** of the students confirmed that they felt like **committing suicide** at least once in the last couple of years. In absolute terms, these are likely to be disturbingly large numbers.

The report reveals that-

63.5% of the students - Reported stress due to **academic pressure**.

66% of the students - Reported feeling **pressure** from their parents and school for better academic performance.

32.6% of the students - were symptomatic of **psychiatric caseness**.

81.6% of students - Reported examination-related **anxiety**.

Further, the National Mental Health Survey 2015-16 reveals that **9.8 Million** Teenagers in the age group **13-17 years** suffer **depression** and other **mental disorders** and are "in Need of active intervention"

Failure in examinations led to **2,413 suicides** by students in **2016** -- or **seven** every day -- accounting for **25** percent of student suicides.

Every day, 6.23 students commit suicide due to peer pressure.

According to the UN report on World Happiness Index 2018, India is at **133rd** Position out of **156 countries.**

No Indian University is even in the top **300** World best university Ranking. Not even a single IIT and IIM.

Expert Talk on the above problems-

"We cannot expect any change in our rankings until the method of teaching is transformed into practical, concept and application based,"	"Our testing and evaluation methods also need to be transformed to measure students understanding and application for creative problem solving."
Parents don't have sufficient time for kids. There's no healthy communication between parents and their children. As a result, the bonding factor is lacking	The popular perception is that failing exams or inability to cope with academics is the primary reason for student suicides

All these figures and reports reveal that there is something wrong in our Indian Education system that we do not understand. Our education system is broken because of not following the complete learning cycle.

Today students and their families are paying thousands of rupees in school and tuition classes where majority of the students are still lacking conceptual knowledge, still not able to clear the exam because of stress and tension, not gaining confidence to face exams, going into depressions, feeling inferior and insecure, keeping themselves away for family functions & social gatherings and doing suicides at the end of day. And we ask you all this for WHAT?

Why are we doing this to our children?

Why we always consider that the development of better computers, smart phones, cars, etc. is more important than innovation in education? We never realized that innovation and improvement in education are as much important as others. For an individual, a nation, and humankind to survive and progress, innovation and evolution are essential. Innovations in education are of particular importance because education plays a crucial role in creating a sustainable future. Today all of the student's problems will only be sought out by involving a combination of new learning methodologies, science, and technology in education.

This is the time that we should redesign learning with keeping today's students and today's technology in mind. There are plenty of multi-billion-dollar organizations in the education space, and we don't believe they are innovating in the way what today students needed them to be and we don't need them anymore. To us, it's really all about the students and we believe the students are not being served as well as they could. They are not provided any training on science of recollection due to which they are not able to complete the learning cycle.

A country's future rests on the shoulders of its youth and children, quite specifically on how they are taught and engaged to think and act.

ROOT CAUSE ANALYSIS - Core Reasons of Confusions / Pressure and Stress

Responsibility to memorize.

Desired competitive marks

Home work- coaching and schools.

Revisions and repetitions.

NO motivation

Less / not interesting

Less time – Huge syllabus

Multi faculties for 1 subject / topic

No clear goals

Incomplete study cycle – all 4 dimensions

Educational psychology not being used.

Absence of GURU in life

More knowledge but Less Skills of Studying

Old methods and Old process of studying

Lack of Innovation in Studies

So many coaching centers SO MANY Students ---Competition

NO SCIENTIFIC APPROACH- Special on RECOLLECTION PART

BrainyWood

What is Brain Science ?

It is based on educational psychology to give psychological solutions to students in order to enjoy the studies and exams. Students usually forget the content even after memorizing so many times. Brain Science deals with removing the habit of forgetting by converting the study content into permanent memory with the help of imagination and association principles.

It is based on Mnemonic science– Recollection science also known as 4th dimension of education.

Education Learning has four dimensions 1. Reading 2. Writing 3. Understanding and 4. Recollection (Nobody is helping students in recollection).

The Time has come to Empower Students with New Scientific Techniques of Learning - Introduce Students with 4th Dimension of Learning !!

READING

WRITING

UNDERSTANDING

Schools, Google, Coaching Institutes, Other Ed-Tech Apps are there

MEMORISATION (No Help to Students in this Dimension)

NO SUPPORT ??

Our Scientific Approach - Why is it Needed?

Today most schools, coaching institutes and even Ed-tech applications are providing only 3-dimensional Solutions – Reading, Writing and Understanding but the student learning cycle gets completed when read, written and comprehended information/study content is finally recollected. In exams, students are supposed to recollect the study content in the form of answers. So this is the area in which students do maximum mistakes and score as per their recollected memories. Students take is as pressure or pain because they are not yet trained on recollection science. Have you ever seen or heard where students are being taught or trained on – How to recollect in exams?

Today this 4th dimension remains the responsibility of student's self-preparation and since students are not trained in this science of recollection they tend to use old techniques like repetition and cramming which results in increasing mental stress, fear of forgetting in examination and anxiety.

Currently, the majority of the Indian students are trying to drive the car with one wheel punctured, which is not repaired till yet. This is like a car with one tyre flat. Can a flat tyre car go long?

Incomplete Learning Cycle of students is the key reason for the most education-related problems like – Stress, Suicidal attempts, Exam phobia, less interest in studies, depression, and forgetting of study content. Our Application is of the first kind which will take care of complete learning cycle of students.

WHAT MNEMONICS CAN DO IN STUDIES?

- Makes studies simpler & interesting
- Increase the speed of memorization by upto 70%
- Increase the duration of retention
- Makes recollection faster and accurate
- Helps in getting more marks by upto 70%

MNEMONICS IN PERSONALITY

- Helps in focus & Concentration
- Reduces Stress
- Increases Confidence
- Enhance Personality
- Leads towards Happier and Healthier Life

MNEMONICS IN CAREER

- Makes competitive exams simpler
- Better teaching and training methods
- Develop interpersonal skills
- Reduction in frequent forgetting
- Jobs and Business Opportunities

WE COMPLETE THE LEARNING CYCLE

The student learning cycle comprises of Reading, Writing, Understanding, Learning/Recollecting. Since childhood students have been taught how to read, write and understand and therefore they do not face any problem in these three but what about Recollection/Learning?

They have never been trained on recollection and hence they always face problems in recollecting subjects. The entire Indian education industry is focused on how to improve the reading, writing and understanding part of students. No one is focusing on recollection due to which the all problems are increasing day by day.

The important of all the four wheels is recollection. Brain Science India completes the education learning cycle - Reading, writing, understanding, memorization, retention and finally Recollection. In India, exams hold such an important part in the education system and what is an exam?

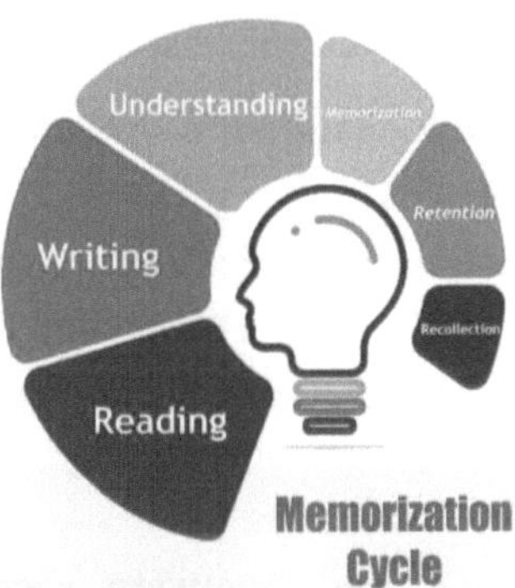

*Based on The New Education Policy

WHY MEMORY and Brain Science TECHNIQUES?

To enjoy a competitive edge in today's cut throat competition and to reduce stress due to examination phobia, scientific methods of study has become very important. We already know what computer has contributed. We know how modern gadgets and technology helping students in their day to day life.

Similarly **Mnemonic** (memory techniques) is a **scientific method** of studies which has immensely helped students in Foreign Nations. It is still to evolve in India. We have a mission on taking an initiative in this field.

WHAT IS BRAIN SCIENCE?

Brain Science – A brilliant and scientific way of learning.

A brain training program based on scientific mnemonic techniques of studying, that helps (student & Individual) in:

1. **Better academic result** – increased exam result percentages.
2. **Faster memorization** -improved and trained memory to reduce the study time and fast memorization of syllabus.
3. **Strong Retention** -no forgetting, permanent memory. Students remember the things not only till exams but till life time.
4. **Quick and accurate recollection**- No mistakes in exams because of accurate recollection.
5. **Development of Holistic Success Skills for Life-**

Not only academics result improvement but skills development for great life and desired success.

What is the secret behind brain science?

- Brain science is basically based on principle of association and power of imagination which are told in education psychology.

Methods of learning that cover all four dimensions of education.

Education's 4 dimensions:

1. Reading 2. Writing 3. Comprehension and 4. Recollection

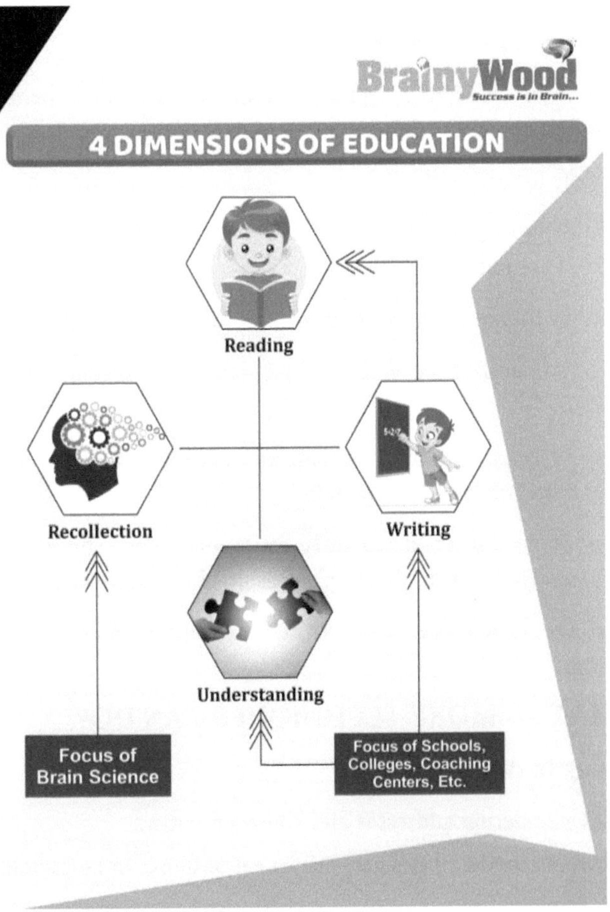

In current education scenario most schools, institutions only cover 3 dimensions – Reading, writing and understanding. But how to recollect in exams, and how to memorize effectively, that is not taken care of so far. So, scoring good marks by covering huge syllabus and memorizing so many things in study have become main reason of stress and pressure on students.

But, Brain Science training develops all 4 dimensions of education for a child by using scientific methods for best exam results without any pressure or stress.

It is **Stress Free Study:**

Have you noticed - Students usually learn in schools or institutes:

1) How to read well.
2) How to write well.
3) How to understand well.

But they do not learn the 4th dimension of education which aims:

How to memorize well & fast - for faster memorization of syllabus.

How to retain longer as well as permanent – so, students never forget anything till life time.

How to recollect accurately and perfectly – So there will be no mistake in exams and exam result will be superb.

And we know the importance of recollection skills in exams.

WHAT MEMORY TECHNIQUES CAN DO?

In day to day life,

1) Remembering addresses and contact numbers
2) Remembering places and placement of things in household
3) Remembering names of people

4) Remembering schedules and appointments

5) Confident Personality

In Academic Life,

1) Memorize your subject Faster

2) Memorize formulas

3) Memorize science equations, periodic table

4) Memorize definitions

5) Memorize Maps and Diagrams

6) Memorize important dates

7) Memorize General Knowledge

8) Memorize difficult words of English vocabulary

9) Memorize theory in points

10) Memorize essays, speech

11) Reduce study time

12) Longer retention

13) Faster recollection

14) Better marks in exams

15) Reduction in examination stress.

World-wide people use eyeglasses for weak eyesight. People go to gym to work out and be in shape and physically healthy. Some people accept that we have weak memory. But what do they do to improve it? There were and are diaries, there are computers, smart phones to help us somewhat. But aren't we helpless without these gadgets? How do you remember important dates, appointments, mobile numbers, locations etc.? And to top it all, how a person appearing in an exam will remember answers to the questions? Will one escape by just saying, "Oh! I am sorry. I forgot"?

In Brain science , I am attempting to give a solution. These techniques have been used world over.

"ALL KNOWLEDGE IS BUT REMEMBERANCE" – PLATO

T- ANALYSIS

	Regular Study Pattern	Brain Science Study Pattern
1	Based only on Three Dimensions of Study	Covers all Four Dimensions
2	Mark sheet Oriented	Holistic Development Oriented
3	Knowledge Based	Knowledge to Skills Based
4	More time to More Marks	Less time to More Marks
5	Only Comprehension Part includes	Comprised of Both Comprehension as well as Memorisation.
6	Audio Memory	Audio- Visual Memory
7	It is in Abstract form	Imaginative Form
8	Left-Right Brain Conflicts	Left-Right Brain Synchronize
9	Slow Memorisation	Fast Memorisation
10	Temporary Memory	Permanent Memory
11	No Futuristic Approach	Based on Futuristic Approach
12	Less Intensity	More intensity

13	Less Scientific	It is a Scientific Approach
14	No Purpose-why and for what studying?	Gives Purpose to Students
15	It is Informative	It is Intellectual
16	Only Reading-Writing-Understanding	Covers- Reading-Writing-Understanding-Memorisation-Recollection-Retention
17	Stressful and Boring	Stress free and Interesting way
18	No fun in Studies	Involves Fun Part in studies.

How to score desired marks by using memory techniques

Highlights -

1. **Interest in studies.**
2. **Increase the result percentage that too by reducing the study time.**
3. **Avoiding mistakes in examinations.**
4. **Empowering retention and recollection skills.**
5. **Self-motivation in self-studies. How to get rid of tuitions and coaching centers.**
6. **Faster memorization, longer retention and quick and accurate recollection in studies.**
7. **Overall development of brain and personality.**
8. **Study online effectively and smartly**

Benefits to Students:

1. Better Exam Results
2. Super-Fast Memory
3. Permanent retention and knowledge
4. Accurate and quick recollection
5. Interest in studies and increased concentration
6. Holistic success skills development.

Key learnings –

1. How to avoid mistakes in exams.
2. Transformation from Confused to Confident.
3. Removing stress and pressure in studies.
4. Science of interest attentiveness in class .Concentration in studies & class room.
5. What to learn -what not to learn, what to study -what not to study.
6. Strategize the exam, Revision plan – for desire marks, Syllabus plan –for covering Syllabus on time.
7. Student –Teacher relation, Student –Principal relation.
8. Four dimensions of study –cognizance, kinesthesis, comprehension and recollection.
9. Habits of student, Innovation in studies. Knowledge –skill -intelligence –wisdom.
10. Time management discipline in studies in life.
11. Mind control techniques. Logical V/s Facts
12. Reducing repetition, revision, study time and increasing result percentage.
13. Synchronization:-mind body –thought & creativity.
14. Being excited about exam, being motivated in studies.
15. How to get Holistic success and being a great personality?

MERIT MADE EASY

With BRAIN SCIENCE – 4th dimension of learning

Have you ever imagined that for how long you have been confused in the web of brain, in the science of learning!

Isn't it strange that we remember some stuff for a very longer period of time and forget some thing which we almost revise daily, for example: the formulas of mathematics or the dates of history!

This is nothing but just the difference between the working of left brain and the right brain. Now the question is how to overcome these problems? How to understand the working of our brain and the science behind it.

For this I came up with a unique concept of Brain Science in which he clarifies the working of our left and right brain and provided different methods to improve the memorization power of the brain and how learning can become easy and fun!

LESSON 1

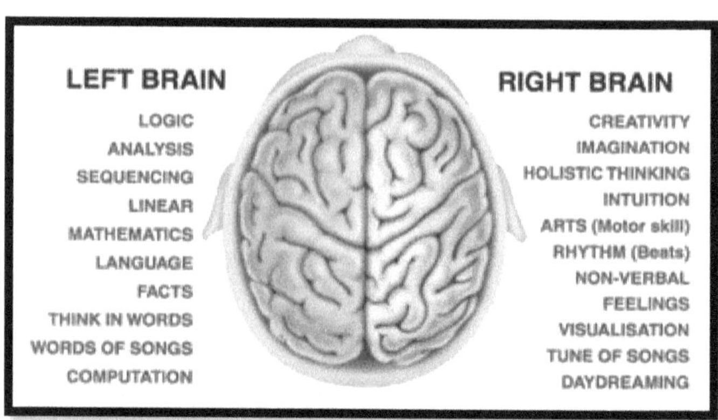

- Brain divided into 2 hemispheres
- 2 halves linked – continuous information exchange
- One half always dominates
- During lifetime average person hardly uses right brain

Human brain is divided into two parts left brain and right brain and the functioning of both left brain and right brain are totally different.

The function of the left brain is to concentrate on Logics, Analysis, Sequencing, Linear, Mathematics, Language, Facts, Think in Words, Words Of Songs, Computation.

Logics- Any particular information which has its basic platform. Things related with logics always have meaning to it. One always learns first, understands and then memorize which stays in our mind for a very longer period of time. For example: we have already studied the Newton's Law of gravity in our childhood where we understood that whatever is held high will fall because of the gravitational force of the Earth. Now as we grow up we do not revise it on daily basis as logically it has been set in our minds that whatever we hold without any support is going to fall! And this information of logic and understanding is stored in our left brain.

Sequencing- This concept is learned and understood by our left brain as what comes after number one is two and then three and so on... or for example we never forget that where our vegetables our kept as we all know they are kept in our fridge but we may sometimes forget that where the keys or the tv remote is kept as they always don't have a fix place and may not be kept in sequence.

Linear- Every thing which includes lines in it like square, rectangle, triangle, etc. This understanding of lines is being functioned by our left brain.

Mathematics- The word 'mathematics' as a subject is the total concept of left brain. Each and every concept which is included in this subject is being performed or controlled and understood by the left brain.

Language- Whenever any new language is learned or understood properly by using correct grammar, when one is capable of reading, writing a language this whole criteria is being controlled by the left brain.

Facts- The permanent memory formed by continuous revising where after particular point of time one does not have to think twice can be known as facts. For eg. "Taj Mahal Is Situated In Agra" is a sentence which every person has heard since their childhood and now this has become a fact! All these facts are stored in the left brain. But one point which has to be noted regarding facts is that the left brain does not store the images related to the facts, it only stores the basic spelling of it. Left brain will not store the image of "Taj Mahal" but only the fact that their exists a word named as Taj Mahal.

Think In Words- Anything related to alphabets, letter, words or sentences being understood by human beings are the work of left brain.

Words Of Songs- Whenever a song is being played, it consists of basically two things, Lyrics and its Tune. The "Words" of the song are being stored by the left brain and not the tune.

Computation- One can say that the left side of the brain is a computer in itself. All kinds of calculation is being controlled by left brain.

Computation- One can say that the left side of the brain is a computer in itself. All kinds of calculation is being controlled by the left brain.

Now, we can believe that all the stuffs like listening, learning, studying, looking, etc. is being done by our left brain. So one will then ask that what is the use of our right brain? So, to clarify that there are so many things which are only controlled by the 'Right Brain' and left brain is not able to do that, let us understand the working of the right brain!

Creativity, Imagination, Holistic Thinking, Intuition, Arts(Motor Skill), Rhythm(Beats), Non-Verbal, Feelings, Visualization, Tune of Songs, Daydreaming, are the contents included in the right brain.

Creativity- Any thing which exist or does not exist, of which a human can think of and can create it . we can say that all the inventions done by so many people is the result of creativity. For example:- before creating an Airplane, Wright Brothers must have first created some picture in their mind and the Ways of it's execution and after that the plane was invented. So all these thinking is stored in the Right Brain.

Imagination- According to 'Albert Einstein' "Imagination" is the most powerful thing in the world. Imagination means watching images in your dream or in the mind which may not be in one's hand but is existing! All the images which one have ever seen or may not have seen exists in the right brain. For example: if just after listening the word 'Airplane" an image of it has been created is the work of Right Brain.

LOGIC ALWAYS COMES AFTER AND IMAGINATION COMES FIRST!

Holistic Thinking- Each and every thing which is complete or incomplete, if any thing is damaged or not damaged, right or wrong this knowledge is known as holistic thinking which is being stored by the right brain. For example: while eating when we taste a food, the realization of the taste that whether the food is tasty or not, this feeling is known as holistic thinking because of which we have a feeling of aspiration being successful in life, making things more perfect, moving towards the success, all this is stored in the right brain.

Intuition- Intuition basically means a feeling which a person feels even before an incident has occurred. We also call it as 6th sense! It do happens many a times that one is thinking about something and that really happens with them, these feelings are basically being controlled by the right brain.

Arts (Motor Skills)- It basically means brain creates a software of the physical working of humans. For example: one must have used smartphones in their life but when it came first typing was a little difficult but after some time our fingers automatically starts running on the keypad without thinking much, but, if suddenly in the middle of the typing one asks to tell that where exactly any particular letter is written we will definitely stop for a second to recognize that whether the letter is exactly written that means the thumb which we are using on the smartphone to type knows where the letters are but not us , this skill is basically known as motor skill, which means each and every cell in our body has a memory which is being controlled and directed by the Right Brain.

Rhythm (Beats)- whenever any music is played or one is listening to any tune or rhythm it naturally happens that one starts moving their hands or legs and start adjusting themselves with the beats, this synchronization with the rhythm is being controlled by the right brain.

Non-Verbal- Any language has two forms that is Verbal and Non Verbal. Verbal means which contains words in it but Non Verbal language includes the feelings or which could be shared without speaking but only with the means of expression. For example : if someone asks you that how are you? And you say that I am Good but you are not smiling so the other person will realize that you are lying. This happens because your words may be saying that you are good but the feeling of expression is recognized by the right brain and creates a sense in someone's mind that you are not actually good. So all kinds of non verbal expressions are being recognized by the right brain.

Feelings- All kinds of expressions like being happy, sad, angry, proud etc. all these feelings are recognized by the right brain. It is very much related to non verbal expressions. Human brain immediately understands these expressions which are not spoken, not written anywhere. All these understanding things are directly controlled by the right brain.

Visualization- visualization means having a video memory, which a person looks through eyes and directly all of that is stored in the right brain. Human being contains overall 7 types of memory, and one of them is the video memory. If right brain would not exist then all the things which a person see would never be able to remember in their life. Turning the visuals into memory is done by the right brain.

Tune Of Songs- One part of the songs is lyrics or words which is being produced by the lyrists , writer of the song and now as we all know that those part of the songs which are being produced in words comes from the left brain but any song is incomplete without its tune. The singer is the one who gives a tune to the song and that tune comes from the right brain. One must have seen that it happens many a times that a singer when performing a song on the stage sometimes forget the lyrics but still continues to sing the tune which means that tunes are much more remembered than words. So all those tunes of the songs goes to the right brain while all the words go the left brain.

Day Dreaming- All kinds of expectations or dreams which a person looks forward to accomplish in his life, all the goals a person sets in their lives, all the expectations for the betterment of life for example: some people wants better house, or better job, better lifestyle, etc. all those dreams are the part of thought process of right brain and the memory for the accomplishment of these goals is set in the right brain.

LESSON 2

BRAIN DYNAMICS-WHAT WE DO!!

(We help you develop a Balanced and Healthy brain)

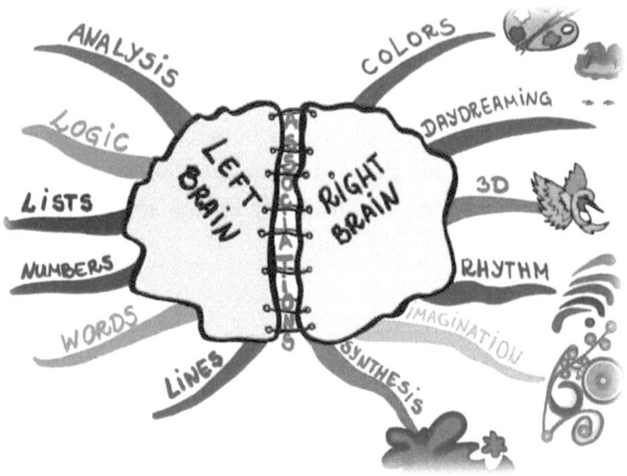

Some people make more use of left brain like scientists , mathematicians, etc. while some make more use of the right brain like writers, painters, musicians, etc.

But the best way is keeping a balance between the left and the right brain. This lesson is all about the fluctuations, concentration and synchronization of brain.

Sometimes left brain does not support the right brain and sometimes right brain does not support the left brain and brain science helps In the association of the left and right brain.

This could be understood by a very simple example from day to day life. Let us say once a mother told her two children named as Chintu and Mintu that today she'll be going out for shopping as tomorrow some guests are going to arrive at their place, so today I am giving you the responsibility to clean the house. If both of you will clean the house properly then I will give you chocolates and will allow you to play in the evening. So the mother distributed the work to both of them as the Chintu was told to clean the drawing room and the bedroom , and Mintu was told to clean the kitchen and the dining room, as, when the guests will arrive tomorrow the mother could say that this beautiful house has been decorated and cleaned by her children. They were bounded by the time limit of three hours. The children promises to do as the mother has said and then she leaves the house. After the mother left both of them got engaged in their respective works and after three hours when the mother arrived the house she was shocked to see the condition of the house as everything was badly messed up in the house, water was splited all over the place, blankets were falling instead of being placed properly on the bed, table and chairs are somewhat broken. In the kitchen water is splashed all over the place, vegetables are lying all over the floor, fridge has been kept open. In the drawing room the sofa set is out of place, all the things in the shelves are fallen down. In short everything in the house was misplaced and destroyed because of which the mother gets extremely angry and calls both of them. They both arrives fighting with each other and the mother gives a slap on their faces and asks the reason behind the chaos. The mother scolds them and says I told you to clean the house in three hours and now the present condition of the house is so worse that it cannot be cleaned even in three days and also tomorrow the guests are arriving. They both started blaming each other. Chintu said that when Mintu cleaned the dining room he kept all the dust in the bedroom and Mintu said that he put all the dust in the kitchen after cleaning the drawing room. So now we can Say that as both of them were responsible for cleaning different things so for the sake of their own work they were trying to destroy the other's work because of which everything became complicated and everything was destroyed. And as a result the timing of the work increased from three hours to three days!! This happened because they had conflict between both of them and so they consumed their tie in two things one- completing their work and second- destroying others work. This also happens with our brain that when left and right brain both are in conflict and a work is given to the brain when it has to use both the sides than the synchronization gets disturbed.

Whenever a person is in tension, they are out of solutions, are forgetting things, cannot memorize any topic on time, forget the faces of people, all these are left and right brain conflicts.

Now imagine that their mother would have given them a good type of training since their childhood and would have made the children understand not to fight with each other so the scenario would have been different and then the mother would have distributed them to work for three hours and after that when the mother would have returned and saw the children playing outside and asked that I gave you work to clean the ask but instead of doing the work you both are playing outside and the children tell the mother to have a look at the house and when the mother arrives inside the room she saw that the house is neat and clean and exactly decorated as guided by the mother. Than the mother asks the children that in how much time you all completed the work and they reply by saying that they completed the work in just one hour. This happened because after you left the house we decided that first we both will clean the kitchen, then we will do the drawing room, and then we will do the bedroom. So this means that they did all the work together. And hence the cleaning of the house was done in less time and was done properly. This is known as synchronization of the brain.

This exactly happens with our brain as whatever our brain learns completely and with full concentration, or when one sings a song with perfect lyrics and tune. This is the synchronization of left and the right brain. If we provide training to our brain to work in all togetherness that means left supports the right brain and vice versa this will result in that one never getting confused, neither the concentration will get disturbed neither will one ever forget anything.

Hence , this is what BRAIN SCIENCE teaches, the synchronization between left and right brain. Brain Science teaches different methods because of which the brain works on all three forms i.e. memorization, recollection, and retention.

In the coming chapters you will be learning the synchronization of left and right brain as this is the most important part of brain science.

LESSON 3

MR. SC. IAS

(BASE FOR A WONDERFUL MEMORY)

Now you are going to read about the **First Memory Principle of Brain i.e. MR**. SC. IAS. The spelling of this word is different as it is an abbreviation. These are some special letters which if one understands fully then it they will be able to use the brain in a complete manner and the brain would get perfect in the science of memorization, recollection and retention.

Let's understand CRISMAS step by step.

So the first letter of the word CRISMAS is ***C***, which indicates **CONCENTRATION**. Since our childhood we have heard, learnt, understood, written, read that if one have to learn anything or have to understand anything properly we need to have a good concentration. We have heard so many times that the teachers are complaining to the parents that the student is fine but it do have a lack of concentration. But the fact is that CONCENTARTION IS NEVER WEAK OR STRONG. It is either CONTROLLED OR UNCONTROLLED. Controlled means that one have the full concentration and Uncontrolled means one has lack of concentration on the brain. Let us understand this properly!

When the students are studying in a class they are having lack of concentration because of which they start talking to each other or instead of concentrating on the topics they open the last page of the book and start typing or making drawing on it. You must have noticed that whenever one is memorizing something after 5 or 6 minutes we start doing something else because we start loosing concentration then again we create concentration that we have to complete a particular topic.

One must have also noticed that we feel to create concentration we need silence place or no disturbance because we believe that a place with silence helps in creating concentration. But one must notice that whenever a child is watching their favorite cartoon or movie on tv, they never get disturbed by the extra noises around them as their total concentration is on the television. No matter if we are sitting in a crowded place but if you are fully concentrated in talking to another person the background sound will never effect you as you are fully concentrated in talking to the person. This happens because the fact is CONCENTRATION HAS DIRECT CONTACT WITH INTEREST and not with silence. In any Particular thing if a person has interest concentration automatically generates there.

We can say that if the study material is not interesting so no matter how much a person tries, they cannot create 100 percent concentration in it. But if the study material is created in an interested manner with a special format then one will be able to have 100 percent concentration in studies as well.

We can say CONCENTRATION AND INTEREST ARE BEST FRIENDS. Let us understand how concentration could be created in studies or we can say how we can create interest in studies or studies could become interesting, let's understand the further meaning of CRISMAS.

The next letter of the word CRISMAS is ***R*** , which indicates **RIDICULOUS THINKING.** This is a very big factor for a good and permanent memory which being discovered my brain science. Ridiculous thinking means weird or different thinking. Things which are extremely different, very unexpected , very weird and is able to make anyone laugh are the things which our brain remembers very easily. For example: if one meets with 100 people it is not possible to remember all the 100 names but if anyone had a name as " Chaparganju" that would be remembered by one for a very longer period of time because it was a different name, a weird name. If one sees a ten feet tall man in a fair, he would be remembered for a very longer period of time as he was different from other common stuff usually found in a fair.

Normally jokes are much more easily memorized than theories as we laugh after listening to jokes. So, if we also make studies ridiculous in our imagination then automatically our studies would become interesting and the concentration power would increase. How this would happen? Now, as you are going to read further your brain without wasting a single second will automatically start to create that images in your mind.

Now let us understand this with some examples : Think of a horse wearing helmet and doing roller skating. So as you read your brain automatically created an image of a horse doing roller skating and wearing a helmet!

Another example could be taken as: Imagine a girl with a hornbill beak instead of a mouth. This means that brain could create those images also which a person has not seen in real life. Brain has a great software known as creativity which could create images while a person is just speaking that in words. Even a computer cannot create things so fast as a person's brain could do so.

Now imagine a rhinoceros wearing a shirt trouser and is hanging from a branch.

Also imagine that you are holding an apple in your hand and as you are about to eat it, suddenly it turns into a monster and that apples opens its mouth with sharp teeth and trying to take out the tongue from its mouth. Now let me ask you a question: from now onwards whenever you are going to eat an apple, will that image would come in your mind or not? This means that your brain could create all that stuff which may have happened earlier, or may never happened. You have ever seen it or may have never seen it, or something is very common or may be extremely ridiculous.

According to the method of MR. SC. IAS. , anything which is Ridiculous and with the help of imagination, all the images would be turned in a Permanent Memory. Which means that in just one time we could remember it for a very longer period of time.

Let us understand **how to apply Ridiculous Thinking in Studies!**

There is a method called **ABC Principle** to make things Ridiculous.

In Brain Science **A means ACTION!** According to Brain Science whatever thing is in motion that means things which are not stable but continuously moving, brain registers those things very fast.

The second principle is B means BIG! Brain registers bigger things faster than the smaller things. For example: In our homes we many times misplace smaller things like safety pins, all pins but we never forget where the fridge or television is kept as they being registered by the brain on some fix places. Even if we shift those things to some other place our brain would remember that at some time the fridge or tv was kept at this particular place. Whenever we go to a new place for example in any hall we remember the big things which one sees but may not remember the smaller things as the brain registers the bigger things faster.

Third principle is C which means COLOR! Things which are colorful in nature, brain registers those things faster. People love watching colorful movies rather than black and white movies. You must have noticed that whenever you go to a clothing shop, you are always attracted to the colorful clothes. If you visit to a salon and we are in a waiting queue and a newspaper and magazine are kept in front of us then what would you choose to pick? Magazine would be your answer as our brain is attracted towards the colors. This is the nature of the brain. If this nature of the brain is joined with the studies which means that without changing the book your books also becomes colorful and full of pictures than studies would automatically becomes interesting, which will make it easier to learn.

With the help of a simple example let us understand the concept of ABC Principle: let us imagine that you went to see a fair and after that when you come home back or even if think of it right now then what is the first thing which comes to your mind? I hope it would be the giant wheel. You will also see other stuffs in your mind remembering the fair but the first thing one would see in their mind would be the giant wheel because it contains all three forms of ABC, first it is in motion, second it is very big, third the giant wheel is colorful as well. Anything which contains all these three principles and you have seen it, then you don't have to remember it but it will automatically come to your mind.

This could be done with anything. Anything could be made Ridiculous with the principle of ABC.

Imagine a bottle which is extremely big and is made up of different colors moving towards you so that you can drink water from it. You must have never seen this in reality but your brain imagined it and made a picture out of it. As you are reading it the brain is continuously creating it in your mind and this is the power of brain. You can also do these exercise by taking different objects for example ice cream, bottle, snake, etc.

Now, let us understand the next letter of the word MR. SC. IAS i.e. the letter ***I,*** which indicates

IMAGINATION (Visualization) . This means that anything which has an image our brain takes interest in those things. One of the most important memory of our brain is "Photographic Memory". With words any photo is attached with it, brain remember that thing faster.

We have two important memory: first is the "Ear Memory" . That means learning by listening. Whenever a teacher dictates and the students listen to it or when we are reading silently but the mind is listening to the words, while we are writing something our brain listens to the words, this memory in which we listen and learn is known as the ear memory or audio memory.

Second is the "Video Memory" ,in which we learn by watching. Learning by watching is twenty times more powerful and easy than listening and then learning. That means our eye memory is twenty times stronger than the ear memory.

In simple terms **50 times Reading, 30 times Writing, 20 times Listening, and 1 time Watching is one and the same thing.** Which hence includes watching is the most easiest method of memorizing.

So, if we convert the studies into imagination, that means study material is converted into images, than that study material could also be watched in our minds with reading and writing which will include that rather than reading for fifty times one only have to watch it ones a time.

But, now the question is how to watch the study material? For that one has to convert their study into visuals which will make the study interesting. We like bollywood movies because we watch them. Now think if you go to a theatre and there you are provided the movie in a book so would you like to read there sitting for three hours? The answer would be No, but that movie if being visualized we enjoy watching it for three hours and we remember that movie as well.

The next letter of CRISMAS is ***S*** which mean ***SLEEP***. Many a times this is said that sleep is the enemy of studies. You must have seen so many students doing late night studies. We have heard this so many times that the more hours one spend on studies, the more result one gets, but the fact is that it is a total myth. Even if you ask a teacher that what should we do to get a good result, the teacher would suggest to do a lot of study. That means to increase the time of study we decrease the time of sleep.

But the fact is that when we sleep our brain does not sleep, rather it reorganize all the information being collected in the whole day! That means the sleeping time of a person is the reorganizing time of the brain. Indirectly if we are also reducing the reorganizing time of the brain.

For example if a non organized room is there and it will take four hours to clean it, but if only one hour is giving for it, then you will be able to organize only those things which takes one hour in it. Just like that when brain is sleeping, that is the time when only your conscious brain is sleeping, it make your goes to sleep so that no new information could be registered in the brain, it stops your conscious activities so that in the sub conscious mind all the information could be organized. But if we reduce the sleeping time than the brain won't be able to organize the information stored because of which mistakes happen with the students in examination!

Many a times this happens with the students that after learning a particular answer many times at night the students get assured that the answer is now learned but still the next day in the morning while attempting the examination the answer is forgotten, this happens because your brain heard the answer, red the answer, written the answer, learned the answer, understood it, revised it, but it did not got the time to organize it properly. Brain was not able to store it, as the storage time was reduced by not sleeping!

Now let us understand that rather than reducing the time of sleep what methods should be applied so that in less span of time we could memorize properly what we have studied. Your moto at the end is to memorize, so there is no need of reducing the sleeping time! For a healthy brain sleeping is very important that too for 8 hours. Sleeping for 8 hours is a very good organizing activity for brain, it keeps the mind fresh, brain works intelligently, it increases the memory power of the brain, memory storage, memory receiving, memory recollection, and memory organizing becomes very easy for the brain to function accordingly. Any information received by the brain in raw form, and when a person sleeps , the brain process it into the organized information which works as as a food for the brain which hence the brain converts it into a form of memory.

To have all this rather than changing the time schedule of studies and sleep, one can change the pattern of study in a limited time by applying the methods of Brain Science which will help you to memorize twenty times faster in the same time period of studying!

Some more important points to keep in mind: Never read a new topic one hour before sleeping and one hour after waking up from a sleep. Rather use that time for revising what have already learnt. Avoid intake of caffeine 4 to 6 hours before bedtime. Never eat any carbs or fatty food before bedtime. Eat anything one hour before bedtime. If before bedtime. Eat anything one hour before bedtime. If you still feel hungry try to eat light food like fruits.

The next letter of CRISMAS is ***M*** which indicates ***MNEMONICS.*** The meaning of mnemonics is RECOLLECTION. The dictionary meaning of mnemonics is Artificial Aid To Memory. Science of brain training which means how to train your brain to memorize faster and for longer period of time i.e. longer retention, and quick recollection. The synchronization of these three science is known as Mnemonic Science.

Different techniques and methods are given which helps to remember different kinds of information. For example we have learnt this in our childhood that if we have to memorize that how many days are there in the months i.e. if the month is of 30 days or 31 days. We use the knuckles of our hands to memorize this. This happened because we took an artificial aid of our knuckles to remember that information. Another example could be used as VIBGYOR, which we use to remember the seven colors of rainbow in series. For that we took the first letter of each color and made a word as V means Violet, I means Indigo, B means Blue, G means Green, Y means Yellow, O means Orange, R means Red.

VIBGYOR as a word does not have any specific meaning in reality but with the help of this word we learned to save our main information. These kind of basic examples are a part of Mnemonics. These are some very basic or primary methods of mnemonics science and there are so many different methods of this mnemonics in brain science which will make you learn in advance manner.

The next letter of the word CRISMAS is ***A*** which means ***ASSOCIATION****(LINKAGE)*. To join one information to any other information the link which has to be used by brain science is Association. Dr. Thorn Dyke has spoke about it several times. Let's understand with the help of an example: There is a train and in that train there are 20 compartments and the first compartment consists of an engine. Which means that the power to move the train is consisted only with one compartment but still all the other compartments of the train move all together, the only reason behind that is the linkage or the association of all the compartments with each other. So if we break the linkage of all the compartments then each compartment would need a separate engine to move on!

The fact of the brain is that, whatever our brain memorizes it always do it with the help of association. Brain is the house of different informations, when one information is associated with another information then it creates memory in the brain. If the association is weak then after sometime the memory will be lost but if the association is stronger between two informations and then the memory will be remembered for a very longer period of time or permanently.

Let us understand the concept of association in a better manner. There is no difference that the information was seen for 1 hour, for 10 hours or it was seen for just 1 sec. What matters is that how the association was created. For example if we talk about common association than we can say the clothes are kept in the almirah. So the association of the clothes is with the almirah, if said that name two movies done by Mr. Amitabh Bachhan than the first thing which your mind will create would be of Amitabh Bachhan and then you will be able to associate him with two of his movies but if you have been given a word as acrophobia then the first thing your brain will create will be spelling of the word and not its picture as the word acrophobia does not have any associated image of it in your brain. So the image of Amitabh Bachhan is set permanently in your brain and because of which it association is very easy as now it's a part of your permanent memory and you may remember the meaning of the word acrophobia, but, not for a very longer period of time as the brain does not have any associated picture of it, so it will be set into your temporary memory. This is the basic work of association, to convert your memory into permanent memory.

Ridiculous Association means link which is created without any logic, which is weird, which in reality does not exist but your mind with the power of imagination can create it.

For example: if a word is said as cricket, so the first thing which comes in mind would not be the spelling of the word cricket but any image related to it for example a bat or ball or the picture of any player for example Sachin Tendulkar. So Sachin Tendulkar is not cricket but as it is linked with the word so our brain automatically associates it with the word cricket, through which cricket is now settled in the permanent memory of the brain. Association makes the recollection easy.

Now let's do some association exercise : let us take some words like Shoes and Trees and try to associate them by creating an image of that in our minds. We will link these two words ridiculously like shoes are hanging on the tree like fruits.

Now let us take four different words and create a single image like cap, bird, ele phant and cloud. Let us say that the image created was like an elephant is there who is sitting on cloud wearing a cap and on that cap a bird is sitting. This does not exist in real but as you are reading the software named as creativity in your brain is continuously creating that. This is what association does helps in imagining, then helps in creating it, and converting it into visual format.

The last letter of the word CRISMAS is ***S*** which indicates ***SCIENCE OF BELIEF!*** Science of belief means to have faith that you are confident in doing a particular work. People many a times believe that they cannot do the work properly because of which the chances of getting failure in life increases. Where as a positive belief increases the chances of success in life. The fact is that belief is in our control and one can belief whatever they may like. In reality we cannot fly but some thought and trusted the belief that humans can fly and they created airplane for that! Trust is very important in life. There are so many things which are limited in life but what we have unlimited is the power of belief! We can think whatever we want to, we can imagine what we want and so we can have belief in what we feel like.

What we trust, belief and approve that forms our personality. Always trust your belief as give yourself an applause for where you are right now and have faith that you can reach many more heights.

Inventions are the result of beliefs! In short we can say that studies could also become easier and there is no chapter in the world which one cannot learn.

Science of belief is a science which says that you have extreme belief anything could become easier and possible to achieve. And if one lives with this belief the chances of success will surely becomes possible. We shall belief that the methods of brain science are very useful and getting 100 percent result is not difficult.

Now let us understand the world of brain science and its applications!

METHODS

The first method is **PIS** ***(PERSONALIZED IMAGE SYSTEM)***

Whatever we like our brain always like to create it as a Permanent Memory. What is the meaning of the word "meaning"? this means that when brain brings any another information with a particular information already given that is known as meaning, or doing association with it.

Meanings are of two types: Personal Meaning and Universal Meaning. Most probably the most commonly known meaning is the Universal Meaning or Dictionary Meaning. And in Brain Science you are also Introduced with Personal Meaning which helps in making learning easier, faster and for a very longer period of time.

PIS or PERSONALIZED IMAGE SYSTEM is a unique system which coverts any word into picture. There are differences in images as some are still images and some are in action known as videos. and in a very strong way brain learns videos very faster, and this is the reason why videos are remembered very faster than studies as they are in action, contains both audio and video and directly impacts the brain.

In universal meaning the meaning of the word is the same for all for example if we take a word BIG, the universal meaning of this word is something which is large. And if asked what image comes when you heard the word Big? Anything could come like any big building, mountain, an ocean, a blue whale, etc. This means that anything which has a specialty of being big will come to your mind.

From this we are concluding that according to the Universal Meaning the meaning of the word Big is Large, but in Personal meaning for every person the image will be different from person to person.

Another example could be taken as Food. Everyone knows it's Universal Meaning as something to eat. But in Personalized Meaning the item which could be eaten would be different from person to person. This means that the associated images which the brain creates after hearing the word as Big or Food is Personalized Image System.

The image that is coming to your brain which is coming automatically and obviously, once you pronounce the word, we will use this image to remember anything which is related to that word. PIS converts unknown words, difficult words or non-pictorial words picture form. Let us understand this better with some examples: all we have to do right now is to learn an original word by associating it with the personal image which comes to your mind. If a word is taken as AGRA, what comes first to your mind? As you heard the word AGRA the first thing which came in mind was TAJ MAHAL. But the fact is that the meaning of the word Agra is NOT Taj Mahal but as Taj Mahal is the speciality of Agra because of which and is a very strong association of it that is why whenever one hears about Agra, the picture of Taj Mahal automatically comes to the brain. So, anything related to Agra could be learned with the help of the image of Taj Mahal.

Creating PIS of any word includes Four Methods which means that if you heard any word and any related image is not coming to the brain, than one can create its own image of it.

1. **RESEMBLANCE**- Resemblance means that if any word is of which the image is not provide than any other related word could be taken with that word, which the brain could make an image. For example we take a word as FERRET. It may be possible that not everyone knows the meaning of Ferret, but you may be definitely getting a related word to it i.e. PARROT. Now if you want to learn the meaning of the Ferret then link it with Parrot. How we will do this we will learn in the next topics in brief but write now let us understand some basics.

2. **BREAKDOWN**- If the brain cannot create the image of any word than break the word into two and the new word which has arrived, create an image of that. For example: there is a word known as KATNI (it is the name of a place), it may be possible that people who does not know this place would not be able to create any image of it in their brain but could only see the spelling. So we can breakdown this word as KATNI: CUT AND KNEE. Two separate words are provided with this as Cut and Knee, through which an image of a broken knee is visible. Now any information if has to be learned with the place KAtNI, the Personalized Image System as broken knee could be used to remember all the information.

3. **SLOW MOTION**- Which means speaking slowly. Let's take a word as ABDICATE. It may be possible that some people may not be able to create any image of it, so if we speak it slowly... we can make a word out of it as : A>>BADI>>CAT. Which generally means (A Big Cat). Right after listening to it an image is created in mind of a big cat. Now if you want to learn the meaning of the word Abdicate and wants to remember it on permanent basis it could be done by linking the meaning to the particular image of a big cat.

4. **Symbolism**- As we earlier talked that when we talked about the word Agra, TajMahal as a symbol came to our mind. Let us take another word as Australia, and right after reading it your brain must have creates the image of a Kangroo, as Kangroo is the symbol of Australia.

Now let us understand what is the use of making these images how they are going to be used by using PIS!

PIS is of two types: BASIC and ADVANCE.

BASIC PIS- Basic PIS is also further divided into two: LHS and RHS. Now LHS contains Already Converted and RHS contains To Be Converted. Let us understand this in a simpler form. What we do in brain science is, if we are reading a theoretical part is that we simply that paragraph by picking the key words from that paragraph, of which images could be made. Then those key words are arranged in such a manner that they are converted into a table, which is known as Simplifying Tablulation. And that table is much easier to learn than the whole paragraph.

Now we divide these key words into two sections as words which are easy an already has an image as for example if we take as airplane, so the image is already converted for this so it will come under LHS that means it is already converted. Now the words which does not have an image and are to be converted for example Let's take a word as Priority. Now after hearing this word it may not be always possible to create an image instantly so this will come under RHS as this has to be converted. Our main focus is on the section which is to be converted, after that to memorize the paragraph we use association method. In any sentence, it contains major key words and others are the filler words. For example if there is a sentence like I drink warm water at 4:00a.m. in the morning. So the key words in this sentence are 4:00a.m and warm water.

The first concept of brain science is to convert any content into a table.

S.NO	INVENTION	PIS	INVENTOR	PIS
1.	Telephone	Telephone	Graham Bell	Garam Bell
2.	Type Writer	....	Christopher Sholes	Shawl
3.	Telescope	....	Galileo	Gali, Leo
4.	Radio	....	Marconi	Maar, koni
5.	Sewing Machine	....	Elias. B. Howe	Laash, Home
6.	Lift	....	Elisha Graves Otis	Alisha, Grapes, Roti
7.	Electric Bulb	....	Thomas Alva Edison	Thermos, Halwa
8.	Aero Plane	....	Wright Brothers	Write, Brother

Now with the help of example of a table of Inventions and Inventors, we are going to memorize the names.

The invention is TELEPHONE and the INVENTOR is GRAHAM BELL. Now telephone is included in LHS as we already have an image of telephone in our minds. But we now want to convert Graham Bell into an image that is why it is included in RHS. Now by using the ridiculous method we will convert it as first take the word Graham, the related word which could be linked with it is GARAM(hot) and for Bell we will take the image of a bell. So now we have an image of Bell which is hot. (Garam Bell). Now we will associate it with telephone as whenever telephone rings it becomes hot. With this both LHS and RHS could be learned easily.

Invention is Type Writer and Inventor is Christopher Sholes. We already have an image of Type writer now we will convert Christopher Sholes as from Christopher we can make Christ Offer and with Sholes we can make Shawl (a blanket- used to cover oneself in winters) so we can imagine as your typewriter is feeling cold and Jesus Christ is offering a shawl to it.

Invention is Telescope and the inventor is Galileo. Now we will convert Galileo with the help of break down as we will break it s Gali and Leo and now we will create an image of a gali (small colony) and in that the animal Leo is moving and he is trying to find you by using his telescope.

Invention is Radio and inventor is Marconi. We will convert Marconi as break down ways as we will divide it into two words Mar and Coni. And we will create an image as Mar(to beat) and Coni as Kohni(elbow). Now the image is created as your radio was not working so you started using your kohni you started beating it.

Invention is Sewing Machine and Inventor is Elias. B. Howe. Now we will convert Elias.B.Howe as we will convert it with any related word as Elias as A Laash(a dead body) B as bhi (too) and Howe as home. So the image created would be as there is a dead body at home and that body is sitting and stitching with the help of sewing machine.

Invention is Lift and inventor is Elisha Graves Otis. Now we will convert the name as we will take a similar word for Otis as office and as using our common sense where is lift mostly found, normally in th offices so we can connect it is lift in office so lift is connected with ot8is.

Invention is Electric Bulb and the inventor is Thomas Elva Edison. We will convert the name as the similar word linked with Thomas could be tharmas (thermos) alwa with Halwa (a sweet) Edison with de de son. (son give me) so the image created would be as you are telling your son that fill halwa in the thermos and give it to you and for keeping it warm you keep it on the bulb.

Invention is Aero Plane and inventor is Wright Brothers. There are two brothers who are writing on the plane that we have created it. So like this we can remember the basic words.

Now with the help of BASIC PIS METHOD we will learn some vocabulary words;

First let us imagine a RIDICULOUS story…

Once there was a saint who was writing something on an anchor sitting on the bus as the bus starts it attacks the cat, besides that was the peak of the mountain on which the bottle of lakme lotion was kept, just after that there was a parrot sitting on the roof of the house and he saying that I am searching for something. Near that house was lying a rack on which the bottle of alcohol is kept. Right near the rack is a kali nari (black woman) who is cooking something for his son. She then gives the son a packet of cream and onion lays and a bottle of coke, which makes him very angry and he throws the coke on phone which then produces a very harsh sound. Near him was standing a boy who is holding burger in his hand and trying to enlarge it. Near it lies a pond in which there is a tortoise on whose shell a car is being kept and watching all this a man wearing a goggle is laughing in a silly manner.

With the help of this story, let us try to find the word given, PIS used and it's meaning.

So the first word we are taking is Anchorite which means Saint. So we made a sentence saying a saint is writing something on an anchor. The next word we are taking is Ambuscade which means to attack suddenly. So from the bus and cat we will make it as Ambuscade and as we read in then story the cat was suddenly attacked. The next word we are going to take is acme which means the peak of the mountain. Now for that we took a similar word as lakme which was kept on the peak of the mountain. Now let us take another word as Ferret which means to search for something. So as there is no image created for the word Ferret, we created a simple word as Parrot because it is a similar word as ferret and brain already has an image of it. And remember what the parrot Was saying.. yes, you got it right. He was saying that I am searching for something. Now, let us learn some more words with their meaning. The next word we will take will be Arrack which means related to alcohol. As we know in the story that there was a rack and on that rack was lying a bottle of alcohol. So for arrack we said it as a rack and associated it with a bottle of alcohol. The another word we will learn is

Culinary which means related to cooking. Now as we read in the story that was a kali nari (black woman) who was cooking something. To remember culinary we took a similar word as kali nari. Than we studied in the story that there was son who was provided the packet of lays of cream and onion flavor and the boy got angry. So from that comes out a word as Acrimonious which means to behave badly. Now for Acrimonious we can say it as with the help of break down method as A cream and onion which is giving us the same sound as Acrimonious. We also noticed in the story that the boy was also provided with the coke and he spills the coke on phone which then creates a harsh sound. So from this sentence a word is created as cacophony which means harsh sound. So to remember the word cacophony we created it as coke and phone. The next word we can learn is Burgeon which means to enlarge. Now do you remember anything from the story? Yes, you got it right that a child was standing with a burger in his hand and was trying to enlarge it. So to remember Burgeon we took a similar word as burger. Now we will learn another word as carapace which means shell of tortoise. Yes we studied I the story that there was a car which was kept on the shell of the tortoise. So to remember the word carapace we created an image of a car and to memorizer its meaning we put that car on the shell of the tortoise. The last word which we are going to learn is giggle which means to laugh in a silly way. So to remember this word we created a man wearing gaugles, so the similar word related to giggle was gaugles. And we imagined that a man wearing them was laughing in a silly way.

S.No	Word	PIS	Meaning
1.	Cacophony	Coke + phone	Harsh sound
2.	Anchorite	Anchor + Write	Saint
3.	Acrimonious	Cream and onion	Extremely bad behavior
4.	Culinary	Kali nari	Related to cooking
5.	Ferret	Parrot	To search for something
6.	Acme	Lakme	Peak of the mountain
7.	Ambuscade	Bus + cat	To attack suddenly
8.	Arrack	A rack	Related to alcohol
9.	Giggle	Goggle	Laugh repeatedly in a silly way
10.	Carapace	Car	Shell of tortoise
11.	Burgeon	Burger	To enlarge

Now we will study about Advance PIS. This is known as Advance PIS because sometimes it may happens that both the words of LHS and RHS both does not have any special images of them. So for that we convert both LHS and RHS into an image. When LHS and RHS both comes under the category of To Be Converted, that is known as Advance PIS. We will learn the names of some Countries and its Capital with the help of a ridiculous story.

Now we are imagining that there was a bank kept in a thali (plate) and near that was a philips bulb inside which money was kept. Near that was an ostrich standing on a veena (an instrument) beside the ostrich was a labour who was beating a bun and the bun was singing (gaana) for help. Besides that there were Bandar(monkey) who ran(bhaga) and sat in a van to eat brownie. Near the van was kept a box of vicks and when it was opened sea shells came out of it. Near that a new pot pot was kept from which baingan(brinjal) came out. Then there was an ape and in both his hands he was having samosa (a dish). Near that was a truck in which a key was kept and it was running on angara(burning rocks). Near that was an ola cab on which butter was kept and mango was trying to eat it. Just beside that was a villa and just below that villa van and auto were standing.

So the first country is Thailand and its capital is Bangkok. As no images are available for both these names we created it as a bank is kept in a thali. So to remember that thali became

Thailand and from bank became Bangkok. The next country is Philippines and its capital is Manila. So to learn that we created Philips bulb to remember Philippines and inside which the money was kept and to learn Manila we took similar word as Money. The next line we took was that there is an ostrich who was stading on a veena. So to remember the country Austria we created a similar word as Ostrich and to remember its capital which is Vienna we created a word as veena. The next line in the story was there was a labour who was beating a bun and the bun was singing(gaana) to help. So to remember the country Gabon, first with the help of break down method we created the word as gaaa, and bun. And to remember its capital as Libreville a similar was created as Labour. The name of the next country is Brunei and its capital is Bandar Seri Begawan. So to memorize Brunie we create a similar word as Brownie and to remember its capital we created a story in which Bandar bhaaga (monkey ran). The next country is Seychelles whose capital is Victoria and to remember this we created a story in which to remember Seychelles we made Sea shells and t remember Victoria we created the image of Vicks. The next Country is Benin whose capital is Porto-Novo, and to remember Benin the word Baingan was taken and to remember Porto-Novo the word New Pot was taken. The next country is Samoa whose capital is Apia. So to remember Samoa we created a similar word as samosa and to remember Apia we created Apes. The next country is Turkey and its capital is Ankara. Now to remember Turkey we created an image of truck and to memorize its capital which is Ankara we created an image of a similar word to Ankara i.e. angaara. The next country is Mongolia whose capital is Ulaanbaatar. To memorize Mongolia we created the image of Mango and to remember Ulaanbaatar, with the help of break down method we create dola cab for Ulaan and Butter to remember Baatar. The last country which now we are going to learn is Vanuatu and its capital is Port Vila. And to memorize this we created the image of a villa where auto and vans are standing. So to remember Vanuatu we took a similar sounding word by breaking it as Van and auto and to remember Port Vila we took the image of a Villa.

Country	PIS	Capital	PIS
Samoa	Samosa	Apia	Ape
Vanuatu	Van auto	Port Vila	Vila
Benin	Baingan	Porto-Novo	New Pot
Gabon	Gaaa, Bun	Libreville	Labour
Seychelles	Sea Shells	Victoria	Vicks
Brunei	Brownie	Bandar Seri Begawan	Bandar, Van
Mongolia	Mango	Ulaanbaatar	Ola , Butter
Philippines	Philips	Manila	Money
Thailand	Thaali	Bangkok	Bank
Turkey	Truck , Key	Ankara	Angaara
Austria	Ostrich	Vienna	Veena

This method is very well used in learning the dictionary as well. This is important to know that there are some confusions which could be created by PIS method. In PIS method we link LHS and RHS but it may happen sometimes that the image could be created multiple times and it is difficult to remember that the particular image is depicting what word. To understand this better we will understand this with the help of an example: we learnt that the capital of Japan is Tokyo. So to memorize Japan we took a picture of a similar word i.e. Paan (betel). And for Tokyo we took a picture of Tokna (someone is disturbing) but if we want to learn the Parliament of Japan which is Diet. Or If we want to learn about the Currency of Japan which is Yen. In this case the basic word Japan is same And its picture which we created of Paan, would remain the same. But, the image of its capital, parliament and currency would change. So that will create confusion in the brain that exactly the picture of Paan should be coonected with the capital, currency or parliament! IF any image has multiple Linkage and to resolve this confusion we are going to learn about ***BIIS*** which means **BACKGROUND INTERFERING IMAGE SYSTEM!**

BIIS means that now to create a difference we will use a background or interfering image. Now we will again come to the example of Japan and we have to learn its capital i.e. Tokyo, for that we did not created any background image and simply made an image of paan and tokna and created an image out of it. Now to learn the currency we will first create the image of the word related to currency lets take the image of a bank. So that when we are talking about any country in relation with its currency the first image that will come to our mind will be of a bank. We will learn the currency of some countries keeping in mind the background image that is a Bank.

COUNTRY CURRENCY

- AUSTRALIA DOLLAR
- AMERICA (U.S.A) DOLLAR
- BAHRAIN DINAR
- BULGARIA LEV

- CANADA DOLLAR
- CYPRUS POUND
- ENGLAND POUND
- FRANCE EURO
- GHANA CEDI

Now you my notice that the name of the countries may be different but the currencies of some of the countries are same, so to clear the confusions we will create images of the country and the currencies using the PIS method, remembering the background image that is BANK. So all the images would be linked to bank.

The 1st country is Australia so to remember the country we can use its symbol, that is Kangaroo. And its currency its Dollar we can use a similar word as Doll. And an image could be created as that a Kangaroo has visited a bank to deposit his Doll. The next country is America and to remember that we can use its symbol as Barack Obama and its currency is also Dollar, so now we already have an image of Dollar that is a Doll. We can imagine this as Barak Obama is also depositing A doll in the bank. Now the next country is Bahrain so using the break down method we can create PIS as Bahar Rain(outside rain) and its currency is Dinar and its PIS could be Dinner. So we can imagine this as that you went to bank to deposit your money and suddenly it started raining outside so you decided to have dinner in the bank itself. The next country is Bulgaria and its PIS could be created as Bull (an animal) and its currency is Lev and its image could be using a similar word leaves. So the image in front of us is that a bull has visited a bank where he is depositing his leaves so that he can use them when he found no food to eat. The next country is Canada and using the PIS method the image could be created of a Can which are empty and we can imagine that all the Dolls which are being deposited in the bank, the cashier was first keeping them in the empty cans. The next country is Cyprus and we can use a similar word as Syrup and to remember its currency we can use an image of a pond. And could create a story as that in the centre of the bank there exists a pond which contains coughing syrup rather than water. The next country is England and we can use a similar word as English and to remember its currency that there was an English teacher in the bank who was not well and hence was using the pond as it contains coughing syrup just to get well soon. The next country is France and we can take a similar word image as Dance and its currency is Euro and a similar word could be taken as Hero. So now you can imagine that in the bank as everyone was getting bored so your favorite hero started dancing. The next country is Ghana and the similar word could be taken as Gana(singing) and the currency of Ghana is Cedi so its PIS could be C.D. Now imagine that your favorite singer is singing a song which has been played in a C.D which was necessary as your favorite hero was dancing.

So this is how as using the background image and associating it with the topics one can never get confused in terms of associations. Just like this any currency of any country could be very easily memorized.

Now with the help of BIIS we would to learn some of the names of Parliament of some countries.

COUNTRY PARLAIMENT

- AFGHANISTAN SHORA
- GERMANY BUNDESTAG
- GREECE HALLENIC
- ISRAIL KNESETTE
- JAPAN DIET
- NORWAY STORTING
- SEWDEN RIKSDAG
- RUSSIA KREMLIN
- SPAIN CROTES

Now the key word in this is Parliament that will create its background image that could be the hall of parliament or the ministers present there.

The first country is Afghanistan and from that we can create an image of a Afghan man wearing turban. The parliament of Afghan is known as Shora, we can create a similar word as shor(shouting). So we can imagine that the Afghan man is standing in the centre of the parliament and is shouting something for his rights. The next country is Germany and its PIS could be created as Germs- many. (that means there are germs present in a huge number). Its parliament is Bundestag which with the help of break down method could be said as Bun Dus(10)Tag. So the image could be created as that in the parliament 10 ministers wanted the bun to eat and so it was told that every bun will be having a tag so to recognize that which bun belongs to whom and when the buns were brought they were all filled with germs and were unhealthy to eat. The next country is Greece and a similar word could be taken as Grease(used in automobiles). Its parliament is Hallenic and for that we can take an image of a hall, it could be the hall of the parliament. So the image would be created as the renovation process is going on in the parliament because of which the walls of the hall are being painted with grease. The next country is Israil and we could take a word a similar word as rail(related to train) and for Knesette we could take the image of a Cassette. So we can create an image as that the railway minister records all his speeches in casettenand put all the cassette in all the compartments of the train. The next country is Japan and its PIS could be created as Paan(beetle) and the parliament is Diet and we can take the PIS as the politicians are on diet. So on a special day the politicians say that on this particular they are on diet and the only th9ing they eat is paan. The next country is Norway and we can create a similar word as No Way. And the parliament is Storting and PIS could be taken as Sporting. So the image created would be that someone demanded the politicians sitting in the parliament that as all the politicians are sitting in the parliament and do es not do any physical activities so in front of the parliament sports ground should be created and as all the politicians heard that, they altogether shouted NO-WAY. The next country is Sweden and we break it down as Sweet-Den. Its parliament is Riksdag and the PIS which could be created as Risk Dog. So the image which could be created as that behind the parliament is a den where sweets are kept which is given to the ministers when they perform well and so that everybody could not reach that den a dog is kept there who is very risky for the normal people. The next country is Russia and its PIS could be created as Rush and its parliament is Kremlin from which we can make its PIS as Cream. So the story which could be created would be today there is huge amount of rush in front of the parliament because the politicians are distributing things related to cream as ice-cream or cream roll, etc. The next country is Spain and its PIS could be created as Pain and its parliament is Crotes from which we can make it as Crore(Million). So we can an image as some politicians are being caught with his million of money because of which he is in extreme pain.

Because all the images created are in relation with the parliament or politicians, so this background image will help you to remember any countries respective parliaments.

The next method we are going to learn is ***LINK METHOD***.

This method converts the complex study material into simpler images and converts the images into the form of stories. This method can also be called as story method or linking method. In popular language it can also be called as Memory Pack System. In this the method subject is shown in visual method and its content is present in a sequence form. Story is the most easiest form of our brain which helps the brain to remember for a very longer period of time. The reason behind that is, first of all the story is present in a visual format. Second reason is that a story curiosity in itself, as it keeps the brain concentrated. Thirdly stories are more interesting in comparison to other subjects.

Now let us understand the meaning of Chain Method and how it is used. Whether a content is in chronological order or in sequence or theoritical answer or any content present in points. Chain method will help in all these ways. Let us understand this with help of some examples:

Some words are given as Photo frame, Scooter, Window, butterfly, snake, sword, Michael Jackson, sofa, gold, tiger, chocolate, pot, tubelight, bird, keys.

Now, if we have to learn all these random words in sequence order what method you will apply? Obviously you are going to memorize it again and again. But rather than doing that we can learn them in a very simple method by using chain method. How.. let us understand!

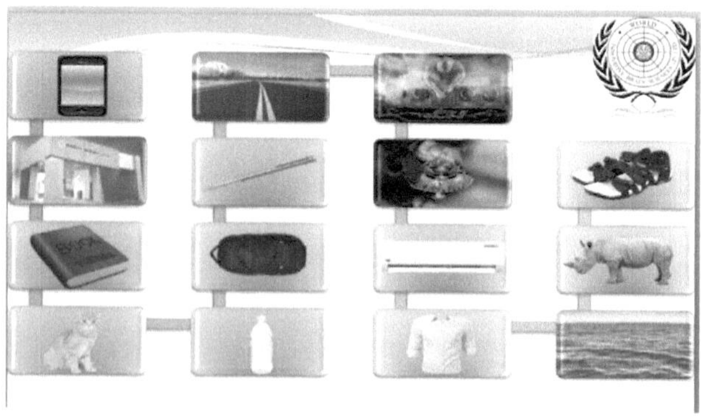

First let us create an image of these words and connect them one by one. So the first word is a mobile . Imagine there is a mobile placed in the showroom, in showroom there was a book, on the book a cat was sitting, a cat was holding a bottle, bottle was kept in bag, from the bag a pen dropped , pen went to a road , over a road there was a DJ, DJ was wearing an earring, Earring was kept over the AC, AC was covered with covered with shirt , there was print of sea over the shirt, from the sea a rhino came out who was wearing sandals.

(THIS IS TO BE NOTED THAT IN THE CHAIN METHOD FIRST ;INK HAS NO CONNECTION WITH THE THIRD LINK AND SECOND LINK HAS NO CONNECTION WITH THE FOURTH LINK. THE CHAIN IS CONNECTED JUST IN THE SEQUENCE ORDER, I.E. CONNECTION 1 WITH 2 AND 2 IS COONECTED WITH 3 AND SO ON..)

Now even if we remove the sequence and you only remember the first word the pictures of all the other words will automatically arrives in your brain. So rather than memorizing the full answer remember the first main word and create the images of all the other words using the chain method.

Now the question arises is that these were simple words whose images are already registered by the brain so what about those words whose images are not created in the brain which eventually is the maximum part of the books. For that we should understand that the content is complicate only till the brain does not have images of it and the only thing on the first hand our brain needs is an image. We have already learnt earlier that how words could be converted in images by PIS method. As soon as you apply PIS method in your content and now you have all the images of your content, with the help of Chain Method you can associate all of them together in sequence and hence it would be very easy for you to memorize all your answers. Let us try to learn the topic of Geography i.e. Layers Of Atmosphere by using Chain Method.

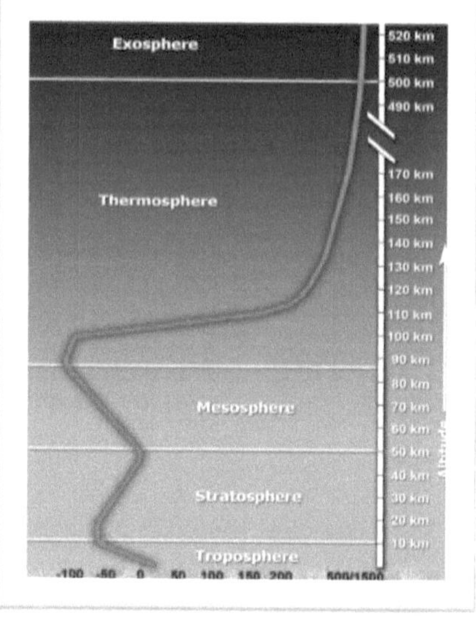

There are Five Atmospheric Layers: Troposphere, Stratosphere, Mesosphere, Thermosphere and Exosphere. Now to learn that we will first create a PIS of all these words. If you look at the spellings carefully you will notice that in these spellings "sphere" word is common, so we will remove the sphere word from all the spellings. So now we are left with Tropo, strato, meso, thermo and exso. Now this is not important that these words are visible or you have any images of it. But with the help of PIS we will create images of these words. Like the first word we have is Tropo and we can take a similar word as Trophy. Now you already have an image of trophy in your mind. And from strato we can take a similar word as straw, the next word is meso and from that we can create its PIS as mazza. The next word is thermo from that we can create an image of tharmas(thermos) and the next word is exso and from that we can create an image of an exhaust fan. Now we can create a story out of it as imagine that you came 1st in your examination and for that you was awarded with a trophy in your school, and as you opened the trophy there was a straw kept in that. And looking at the straw you thought of drinking maaza, and as you was about to drink that mazza your teacher came to the class, so you got afraid and you pour the maaza into the thermos(thermos). But your teacher caught you and she threw the thermos away. She missed her shot into the dustbin, and rather than the bottle reaching to the dustbin it went where the exhaust fan was present and because of it the exhaust fan was present. Like this you can memorize any sequence like this.

Now we will take a topic of history and would try to learn the answer by using chain method. We will learn the names of Sikh Gurus in the sequence order.

***(This is very important to note that this example of Sikh Gurus is just taken to clear the method of Chain method. We respect the dignity of all the Sikh gurus. This example should be taken in a very positive**

manner, just to learn the methods of Brain Science in a better manner.)

There are 10 Sikh Gurus.First we will listen a story as your Nana ji(Grandfather) is eating angoor(grapes)and those angoor(grapes) are sold by Aamir Khan, and Aamir Khan is standing in Ram Mandir (ram temple). At that time ram bhagwan(lord ram) is teaching Arjun that how to use teer(arrow). Arjun shot the arrow which went to the kitchen where your mother was cooking and it struck the vegetable which was Hari Gobhi(Green cauliflower). As the arrow struck the Hari Gobhi the vegetable chopped automatically after which your mother sprinkled hari raai(green mustard seed) on it. This vegetable was being prepared for hare krishan bhagwan(lord Krishna) who is sitting in your drawing room. When he saw that the vegetable is being prepared with the help of teer(arrow)for that he complimented your mother and gave her a tag of being very bahadur(brave). And your mother became very happy and started enchanting or praising hare Krishna as -Hare gobinda hare gobinda(oh my dear lord).

Now if we revise this story as the visualization if this story has now been done I your mind so it will be easier for you to remember that what your nanaji was doing? Yes you are right he was eating angoor, and so on.. now you will notice that the first name was Nanaji from that we can remember the first nme of the sikh guru i.e. Shree Guru Nanak Dev. Nanaji was eating Angoor and from Angoor we could remember Shree guru Angad Dev. The next word is Amir and from that we could remember Shree Guru Amar Das. The next word is Ram Mandir and from that we could remember Shree Guru Ram Das. The next word is Arjun and from that we could remember Shree Guru Arjun Dev. The next word is Hari Gobhi and from that we could associate Shree Guru Har Gobind. The next word is Hari Raai and from that we could associate Shree Guru Har Rai. The next word is Hare Krishna and from that we will remember Shree Guru Har Krishan. The next word is Bahadur and from that we can associate Shree Guru Teg Bahadur. The next word is Hare Gobinda from which we could remember Shree Guru Gobind Singh.

We are now going to understand a very interesting theme, which is known as ***Numeric Mnemonic.*** Now let us understand what NM basically is:

- **Makes numbers pictureful**
- **Memorize long list of words/objects**
- **Helps to memorize each word in its original sequence**
- **Makes random recalling very quick**
- **Helps to memorize a list of up to 60 objects sequentially**

This is basically divided into two parts: **Numeric Mnemonic and Phonic Mnemonic.**

Numeric Mnemonic further consists of three techniques

- HARMONY
- FIGURE AND FEATURE
- SYMBOLIC

[THIS IS IMPORTANT TO NOTE THAT IN NMM METHOD WE FOCUS ON THE NUMBERS FROM 0-20. THIS MEANS IT INCLUDES SINGLE DIGITS AS WELL].

#(Single digits are not used in Phonic Method. Paired Digits are used in the Phonic Mnemonic Method.)

WE ARE NOW GOING TO LEARN ABOUT THE HARMONY METHOD ALSO KNOWN AS RHYME METHOD.

Now, we are going to learn a Very Interesting Method which is going to help you in learning Difficult questions very easily. And the name of this method is ***HARMONY METHOD.***

- A simple Nursery Harmony Method
- We assign each digit from 1-20 a particular rhyming image or picture

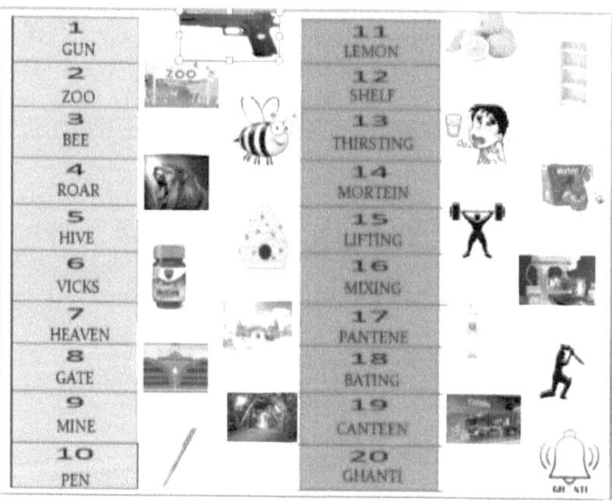

HARMOYNY means rhythm, or we can say a similar ending sound. We have grown up hearing rhymes. Specially in our Nursery classes. Songs are also learned very fast because with the tune they also have rhyming support. We will learn all the name of the Prime Ministers of India till date with the perfect numbers that after which prime minister came whom! From the time of Independence there has 18 Prime Ministers overall. But most off the people remember the present or the first prime minister of the country. But most of the people are not able to remember to remember all the Prime Ministers of India.

With the help of Harmony Method you can remember all the names of the Prime Ministers in sequence, and even if someone asks the name of any Prime Minister from the start or from the end or from the centre. You would be able to remember all of them. Let us first have a list of all the Prime Ministers in series.

1. Jawahar Lal Nehru
2. Gulzarilal Nanda
3. Lal Bahadur Shastri
4. Gulzarilal Nanda
5. Indira Gandhi
6. Morarji Desai
7. Charan Singh
8. Indira Gandhi
9. Rajiv Gandhi
10. V. P. Singh
11. Chandra Shekhar
12. P.V. Narsimha Rao
13. Atal Bihari Vajpayee
14. H.D. Deve Gowda
15. Indra Kumar Gujral
16. Atal Bihari Vajpayee
17. Manmohan Singh
18. Narendra Modi

We will create an independent memory for each Prime Minister. Almost every one, to learn the names will focus on the names of the Prime Ministers and then try to learn it, and we never focus on the numbers written before that. But in Brain Science we will focus mainly on the numbers written before the names of the Prime Ministers, and will create Rhyming or Harmony with those numbers and then link them with the name of the Prime Ministers.

As we will convert the numbers into images. That means we will use both logics and imagination, which is creating synchronization of both left and right brain.

Let us first convert the numbers into images using Rhyme Method.

The first number is 1(one) from that we could create the image of a Gun. So it becomes one-gun.

Two- Zoo.

Three- Bee.

Four- Roar. (Roar of a lion)

Five- Hive(hive of Bees)

Six- Vix

Seven- Heaven

Eight- Gate

Nine- Mine(where Mining activities take place)

Ten- Pen

Eleven- Lemon

Twelve- shelf

Thirteen- Thirsting

Fourteen- Mortein (a machine used to kill mosquitoes)

Fifteen- Lifting

Sixteen- Mixing

Seventeen- Panteen (name of a shampoo brand)

Eighteen- Batting.

Nineteen- Canteen

Twenty- ghanti(Bell)

Now we will connect these images which we have created with the numbers to the names of the Prime Ministers and will try to make a story.

*(this is very important method to note that

On number one we have created an image of a Gun. And the first Prime Minister is Jawahar Lal Nehru.

So we can say that there is a person named as Nehru who has Lal (Red) Gun in his hand.

Second image is of a zoo and our second Prime Minister is Gulzarilal Nanda. So we can create an image as when the minister entered in a zoo an animal threw gulal on him from behind the jhadi(shrubs) and made him ganda(dirty). So from gul became gulal and for zari became jhadi and from ganda became nanda.

Third image is of a bee and the third Prime Minister is Lal Bahadur Shastri. So the PIS would be created as there is a bee which is of red color and a person named Shastri catches him and hence was given the tag of being bahadur(strong).

The next image is of a Lion who is Roaring, and the name of the Prime Minister is once again Gulzarilal Nanda. Now using the Advance PIS Method we will link the images as when the person named as Nanda went to the zoo he offered gulabjamun(a sweet) to the Lion who was hiding behind the jhadi(bushes) and because of the offer the Lion became angry and started roaring.

The next number is five from which we have created the image of Hive and the Prime Minister is Indira Gandhi. So the PIS would be created as Indira Gandhi went to her garden to take have some honey and ordered the gardener to take out Honey from the Hive, hanging on the tree.

The next number is six from which we have created an image of Vicks and the name of the Prime Minister is Morarji Desai so to remember the name with the help of break down method we will break Morarji into Mor(Peacock) and from Desai we could make Desi(local). So now we can imagine that as you have a desi vicks in your hand and on that vicks there is a picture of mor(peacock) on it.

The next number is seven and the image is of heaven and the name of the Prime Minister is Charan Singh. So the story could be created as, imagine you went to the heaven and saw that there is no God there but instead so many charan paduka(sleepers) are spreaded everywhere. This is how you can create any story of your choice.

The next Prime Minister is again Indira Gandhi and the number is eight from which we have associated the image of a gate. So we can imagine that today Indira Gandhi is going to deliver a speech in your near by hall for which the front Gate of the hall is beautifully decorated.

The next number is nine and the image we have taken is of a Mine, and the Prime Minister is Rajiv Gandhi, so to remember Rajiv Gandhi we can create an image as from Rajiv we can make the word as Raja(king) and for Gandhi we can create an image of Mahatma Gandhi, and can imagine that Mahatma Gandhi has ordered the Raja of a place to go and have a visit in a mine so to check that the work is properly done or not.

The next number is ten and the related word is Pen. The name of the 10th Prime Minister is V.P Singh. Now we can remember it as there was a Singh(lion) who was renowned as V.I.P in the jungle as he was the only one who knew how to write with a pen.

The next number is eleven and the image we have created is of a Lemon. The name of the 11th Prime Minister is Chandra Shekhar. Now we can create story as, imagine you asked your mother that you want to drink lemon juice and your mother replied that from now onwards lemons are not available on planet earth and if you want to drink lemon juice you have to go the chandrama(moon). So for that you went to the chandrama and there you saw that the lemons are now available on the Shikhar(top of a mountain peak) of the moon.

The next number is twelve and the image is of a shelf. And the name of the Prime Minister is P.V Narsimha Rao. From Narsimha Rao we can relate him with lord Nar Singh. So you can imagine that you have a picture of Narsingh in your shelf.

The next number is thirteen and the related image is thirsting. And the name of the Prime Minister is Atal Bihari Vajpayee. Now imagine that Atal Bihari Vajpayee has visited your home and he was feeling very thirsty so you gave a glass of water to him and for that he said thank you.

The next number is fourteen and the image we created is of Mortein(a mosquito killing machine). And the name of the 14th Prime Minister is H.D. Deve Gowda. First of all we can create an PIS of the name as imagine you are sitting in a room and watching a scene in your HD quality t.v that there is a Dev(lord) who is sitting on a Ghoda(horse) (so from Deve became Dev and from Gowda became ghoda) and sitting on a ghoda he is running behind a big mosquito carrying a mortien mavhine in his hand just to kill the mosquito.

The next number is fifteen and the related image is of lifting. And the Prime Minister is Inder Kumar Gujral. So we can say that lord Indra is doing weight lifting in a gym.

The next number is sixteen and the related image is of a sewing machine. The 16th Prime Minister is again Atal Bihari Vajpayee. Now we can imagine that Atal Bihari Vajpayee is stitching the national flag with the help of a Sewing machine.

The next number is seventeen and the image is of a panteen(a brand selling bottle of shampoo) and the name of the next Prime Minister is Manmohan Singh. So the image could be created as DR. Manmohan Singh uses panteen shampoo to wash his hair.

The next number is eighteen and the image is of Batting. The 18th and the current Prime Minister is Narendra Modi so we can imagine that Narendra Modi loves pla ying cricket and right now he is doing batting in the cricket field.

Now if you revise all the numbers and the related images and once gain read all the Prime Ministers and remember the PIS created from it. You will never forget all the names of the Prime Ministers in their series.

With the help of this method you can revise anything containing 20 points in it.

The next method we are going to learn is ***FIGURE AND FEATURE METHOD***

- We consider shape of the digits from 1-20
- These shapes are associated with learning points

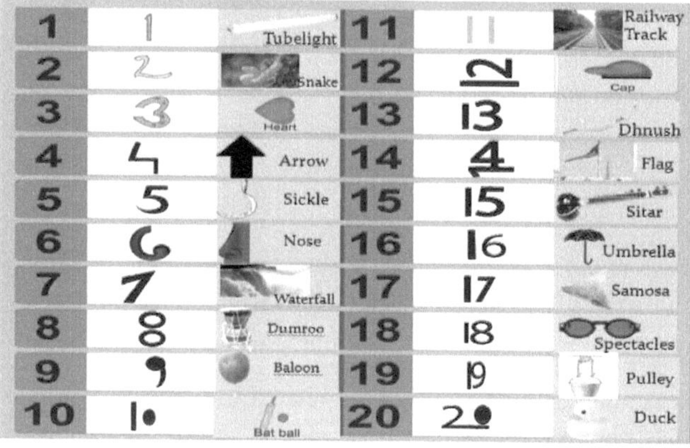

1	1	Tubelight	11	11	Railway Track
2	2	Snake	12	12	Cap
3	3	Heart	13	13	Dhnush
4	4	Arrow	14	14	Flag
5	5	Sickle	15	15	Sitar
6	6	Nose	16	16	Umbrella
7	7	Waterfall	17	17	Samosa
8	8	Dumroo	18	18	Spectacles
9	9	Baloon	19	19	Pulley
10	10	Bat ball	20	20	Duck

Now let us understand this in detail the working of Figure and Feature Method.

In this method we create an image of the numbers according to the shape of the number. We are using numbers from 1to 20. Let us understand how.

Write now you can see the pictures in which an image is created in front of every number. Number 1 has been shown as tubelight. Number 2 has been shown creating the shape of a snake. Number 3 has been shown creating an image of a heart.. and so on...

With the help of these shapes we will learn the names of the Presidents of India that too in series. Let us first know the names of all the Presidents till date.

1. Dr. Rajendra Prasad
2. Dr. Sarve Palli Radhakrisnan
3. Zakir Hussian
4. V.V. Giri
5. Nyay Murti Muhammad Hidayatullah
6. V.V. Giri
7. Fakruddin Ali Ahmad
8. B. D.Jatti
9. Dr. Neelam Sanjiva Reddy
10. Giani Zail Singh
11. R. Venkataraman
12. Dr. Shankar Dayal Sharma
13. K.R. Narayanan
14. Dr. A.P.J. Abdul Kalam
15. Shri Mati Pratibha Devi Singh Patil
16. Shri Pranab Mukherji
17. Ramnath Kovind.

So the name of the 1st President is Dr. Rajendra Prasad and the image of number 1 is tubelight. We can first create PIS of Rajendra Prasad as Raja Ka Prasad. And we can connect it with tubelight as that in his kingdom electricity was supplied for the first time so he decided to give one tubelight in each house of his kingdom.

Now, the 2nd President is Dr. Sarve Palli Radhakrishnan and the image for number 2 is in the shape of the snake. Now from the name of the President, with the help of break down method we can create the image of Radha and Krishna and can imagine that Lord Krishna is having a snake around his neck.

The 3rd President is Zakir Hussain and the image of number 3 is of heart. So from this name we can imagine a very famous Tabla Player Mr.Zakir Hussain and we can imagine that he is playing the instrument tabla which is of rather being round in shape, It is present in heart shape.

The 4thPresident is V.V. Giri and the image of number 4 is of an Arrow. Now we can use Ridiculous Method as from V.V. Giri we can make Biwi giri. (wife fell down). And the reason wa because she was shot with an arrow she fall down on the ground.

The 5th President is Nyay Murti Muhammad Hidayatullal and the image of number 5 is of a sickle. So the PIS could be created in such a manner as, to remember the name of the President we can say Nyay (justice) and murti (statue) and we can create image of saint Mohammad and from Hidayatullal a word Hidayat (in the eyes of) could be taken. So we can create the story as Saint Mohammad is carrying the statue of justice and in the hand of the statue is a sickle and looking at the statue of justice Mohammad is saying that everyone is equal in the eyes of God.

The 6th President is again V.V.Giri and the image of number 6 is of a Nose. Now we have already created a PIS for V.V.Giri as Biwi Giri and the moment she fell off she just broke her nose badly.

The 7th President is fakruddin Ali Ahmad and the image of number 7 is of a waterfall. So the PIS could be created as we can imagine that there is a Fakir whose name is Ali and he is sitting near the waterfall and meditating.

The 8th President is B.D.Jatti and the image of number 8 is Dumroo(an instrument), so the PIS could be created as, from the name B.D. Jatti we can create a similar phrase as Bedee Jali(burning of cigar) and as it happened you became very happy and started playing dumroo.

The 9th President is Dr. Neelam Sanjiva Reddy and the image of number 9 is of a Balloon so from the word Neelam we can create a word as Neela(blue). Imagine there is a balloon which is of blue in colour and there is a doctor named Sanjiv who is getting ready so that he can go out and buy a blue coloured balloon as his child is crying to get that.

The 10th President is Giani Zail Singh and the image of number 10 is of a Bat ball. We can imagine that any gyani person (a knowledge person) who will play bat ball will be punished and hence put to jail. We created jail from zail.

The 11th President is R.Venkatraman and the image of number 11 is of a Railway Track. So the PIS could be created as first of all using the Break down Method we can create an image of Venkatraman as Van Cut Ram. So we cn imagine that on the Railway Track a Van was was running and suddenly the van gets cut into two parts and from inside the van suddenly Lord Ram appears.

The 12th President is Dr. Shankar Dayal Sharma and the image of number 12 is of a Cap. From Shankar we can create an image of Lord Shankara who is filled with daya(mercy) in his heart and now think you gifted him a cap and he excepts and wears it and after weariing the cap, Lord Shankara is now blushing(Sharmana).

The 13th President is K.R.Narayanan and the image of number 13 is like a Dhanush(Bow). So from Narayan we can create an image of Lord Narayan and can imagine him using a bow and arrow.

The 14th President is Dr.A.P.J Abdul Kalam and the image of number 14 is of a flag. Now imagine that Dr. Kalam is hoisting the National Flag of the country.

The 15th President is Shri Mati Pratibha Devi Singh Patil and the image of number 15 is of a Sitar. Now we can imagine that in the Rashtrapati Bhawan Shrimati pratibha patil is Playing with a Sitar(an instrument).

The 16th President is Shri Pranab Mukherjee and the image of number 16 is of an Umbrella. Now the PIS could be created as imagine that whenever Shri Pranab Mukhrejee is arriving at the Rashtrapati Bhawan he always carries an Umbrella with him.

The 17th and the present President is Ramnath Kovind and the image of number 17 is Samosa (a dish). Now we can imagine that there are two brothers named as Ram and Govind (similar to Kovind) and they always eat Samosa before going to the Rashtrapati Bhawan.

We just learnt the name of all the 17 Presidents. Now you can tell any known person to ask this series from you. You will realize by just remembering the codes you would be able to instatntly recall the names of all the Presidents that too in series vice.

PHONIC METHOD

This method is for those who are often confused with numbers. And it his hard for them to remember the numbers. In mathematics we have numbers, square root, cube root, multiplication tables, etc. in science we have atomic mass numbers, melting point, boiling point, etc. in history we have dates of different occurrences. Someone wants to remember the birth dates of people, etc. in short at any point if you want to memorize anything related to numbers then Phonetic method is a very useful method for you.

Digit	Letter
0	S
1	T, D
2	n
3	m
4	r
5	L
6	J, g
7	K
8	f, v
9	P, b

Now let us understand what it is and how it is used!

All the numbers are been made from 0 to 9. And Phonic method converts numbers into picture method. We can say that a number is a number and any picture consists its particular name that means it consists of letters from a to z. So from those letters a word would be created and from those words a picture will form.

You can see the picture where in front of every number a letter is written. This table is known as the Phoneic Table. Now let us understand the meaning of this table.

First off all these letters are given in such a way that they are somewhat related to the image of the number. And secondly these letters are taken because according to the methodology of Brain Science these are the most common letters used to create any picture.

One thing is also to be noted that this table does not contain any vowels. All these letters are just consonant letters. According to Phonetic science vowels work as a cement whereas the consonant letters works as bricks which altogether creates a building. Take any consonant word and write any vowel before after or in between the consonant letter that will create a word most commonly.

In brain science we does not have to use any much logic, this is a creative work. So while creating any picture or a word it is not necessary that you keep the basic fundamental principles in mind like the exact grammar or anything.

Now in the table in front of 0 a letter is given that is S, so how we will remember it. What we will do is we will imagine that we have cut 0 into two parts. Now you will get two hemispheres from it. No while adjusting these two hemispheres we can notice that we have got a shape like S.

The next number is 1 and the letter we have is 1 and the letters we have are T and D. the letter T is taken because it is somewhat similar to number 1 and D is taken because the basic sound of the letter D is similar to T. They belong to the same class. In both these letters we are folding our tongue and touching the palate. We have kept D with T as a substitute so that if any word is not available with the word T then you can make it with the word D. D can be used as an alternate.

The next number is 2 and the letter we have used is small 'n'. Just observe the shape of number 2, if we turn it then it will look like small 'n', that is why we have taken the letter 'n'.

The next number is 3 and the letter used is small 'm'. If you make the number 3 stand then it would look like small 'm'.

The next number is 4 and we have taken the image of small 'r'. we can remember this as, we call number 4 as 'chaar' in the hindi language. So it can create a rhyme as chaar- r. and if we look at the way of hindi counting number 4 is also drawn like r. so we can relate it in that manner.

The next number is 5 and we have taken the image of letter L. now as not much of an image was available for 5 so what we did was when we look at our hand and someone tells us to show number five so we open our full hand and show all the five fingers. Now, if we deeply notice our thumb and rest of the fingers they make a shape like L.

The next number is 6 and the letters we have taken is small 'j and g'. We have taken small j because if you notice number 6 and turn it, then it will somewhat look like small 'j'. And g is taken as an alternate to j, as both of them comes from the same sound origin.

The next number is 7 and the letter we have taken is K. the letter K is taken because if you notice you it could be seen that on number 7 another 7 is kept. So it looks like K.

The next number is 8 and the letter we have taken is small 'f and v'. If we write f in cursive writing so it looks like we have open 8. And v is taken as an alternative as two v joined together up and down can make an 8.

The next number is 9 and the letter taken is P and small b. This could be taken as if you look 9 in the mirror than it would look like P. and P and b has similar sounds.

How to make Phonic codes:-

Example: 01

0 means S and 1means T. so we can add the vowel in between these two numbers as UI and we can create the word as Suit.

Some exceptions like 77

So the letters we will get will be K and K. so we can make the word as kake. Now the exact spelling is Cake but in brain science we do not use logic and we just want to create an image out of it. So the correct spelling does not matters.

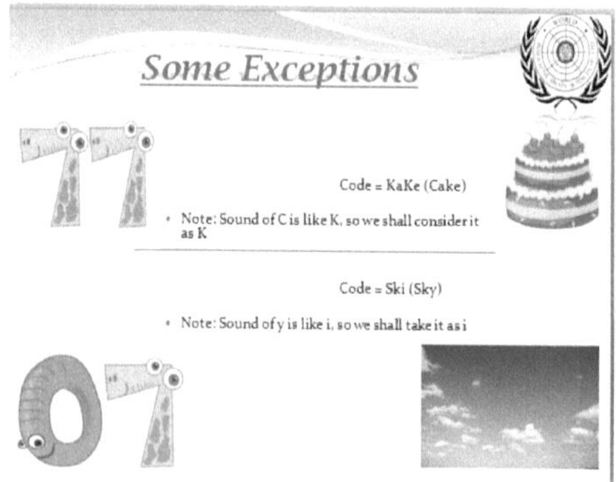

The next method we are using in the Phonic Method is the VIBGYOR Method. We are using this to remember the dates of history.

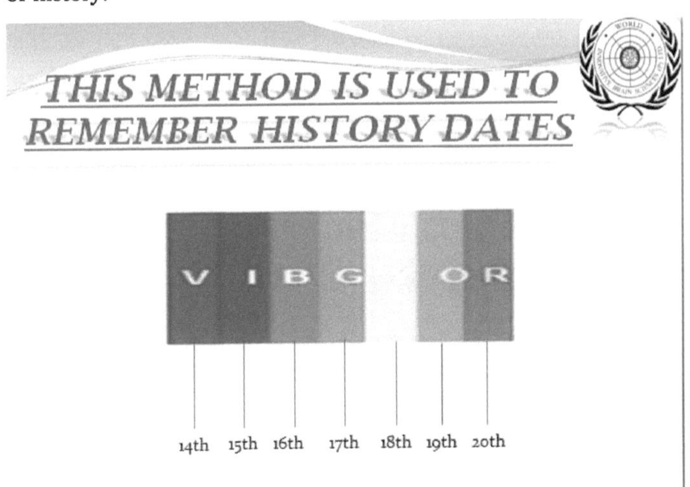

For example if we want to remember the birth year of Mahatma Gandhi i.e. 1869. The first thing to notice is that there are two things in the birth year of any person first is the century and second the year. So we noticed that the most common used centuries are 14th 15th 16th 17th 18th 19th and 20th. So rather than writing or making different pictures for them again and again we used VIBGYOR Method and named each colour with the century. 14th Century- violet, 15th- Indigo 16th- Blue 17th- green 18th-yellow 19th-orange 20th- Red.

Now remembering the dates would become easier for you as you only have to convert the year and not the century.

Now, we can create an image as 18th century refers to yellow colour and 69 refers to alphabets J and P so from that we can make a word as Jeep. We can imagine that there is a Jeep which is yellow in colour and is fully decorated with balloons and Mahatma Gandhi is riding the jeep. So this is how you can remember the history dates very easily.

DIAGRAM METHOD BASIC

Lets take a situation when you need to learn biological diagrams:-

The approach to to train the memory to handle the biological diagram is just amazing.

- Used to memorize unlabelled diagrams
- Look at the shape and try to find identify a known image from it.
- Look at the name and make PIS
- Associate the two.

Let us understand these points with an example:

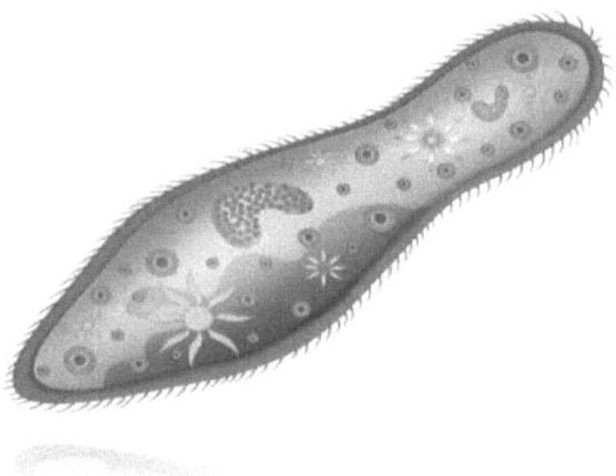

Now, look at the shape of a Paramecium cell. The very first glance gives you a hint that it looks like a slipper or a shoe. So, it would have been better if it was named as a 'shoe' or 'slipper cell'. But scientists named it as Paramecium. So the PIS could be created as I am wearing a paragon Slipper. Paramecium- Paragon/per(leg)

DIAGRAM METHOD ADVANCE

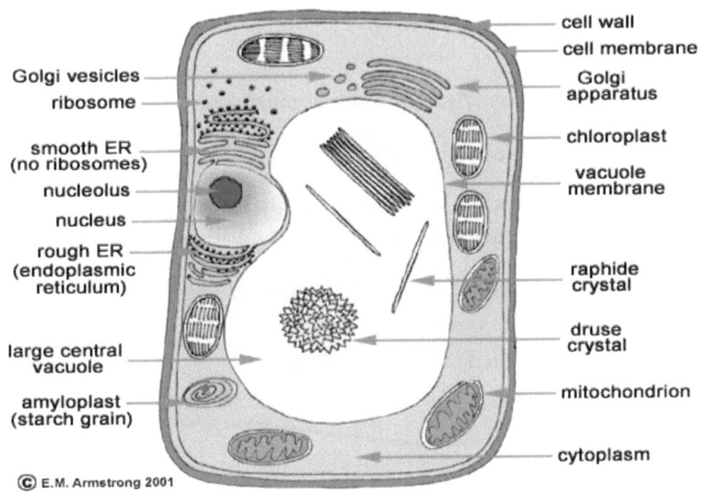

The immediate thing which may strike in our mind while looking at the diagram could be a mental picture of a big ground surrounded by walls at all the four sides with a swimming pool.

Now, look at the naming starting from the word 'starch grain' and link them with the visual words which come in our mind.

Original Substitute

Starch grain Torch

Vacuole vacuum

Tonoplast Tin and Plastic

Mitochondrion Meeting and cone

Golgi apparatus Gol*(round) apparatus

Chloroplast Coloured Plastic

Endoplasmic End-plus(sign)

Reticulum Rat

Ribosome Some-ribbon

Nucleoplasm Nakli*(imitation) plastic

Nuclear Envelope Nuclear furnace and Envelope

Nucleus New-class

Cytoplasm Seat

Plasma membrane Member holding plus(sign)

Cell wall Wall made up of cells.

We can memorise the diagram easily by fabricating a funny and interesting story by joining all the words together.

We can memorization of biological diagram fun by comparing its shape and some similar looking picture and then linking its naming with a ridiculous or logical story.

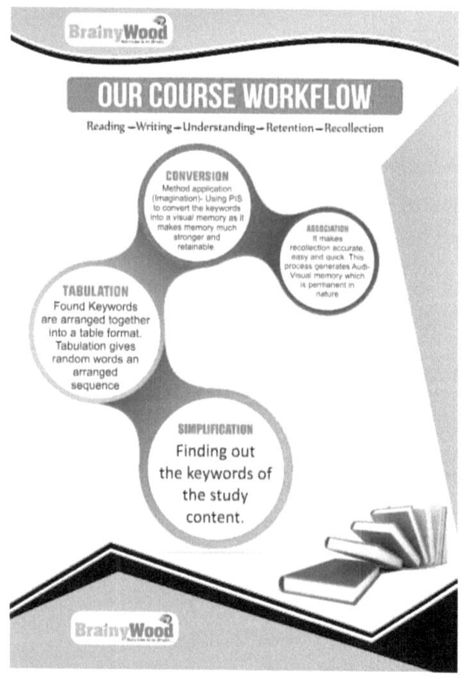

THE SECRET OF REVISION

WHAT IS REVISION

You must have been asked to do revision by your teachers so many times. If we want to make the study content memorized usually we are advised to do revision right!

But do you know the exact meaning of revision? Most people think the meaning of revision is , reading and revising the content again and again so as to make it stout. BUT revision is something different , yes it is important to do revision if we want to make memory permanent but that it not reading multiple times.

In previous chapter s of the book we came to know that our strongest memory or information format is video or visual memory or eye memory. Which means what we can see is the best memory.

What we use to see – EYES right!

EYEs are also called vision. Moreover, eyes are used to see the things physically.

But if we want to see the things mentally, it is called our vision.

We are advised to have Vision in life, Life's vision means what we see in our future.

Which means physically or notionally Vision is most important.

VISION means seeing for first time. REVISION means seeing gain , look at this word

REVISIOJN = RE-VISION that means vision again, seeing again. Seeing again, not reading again. But students while doing revision they just re-read the content. Actually they do not make the study visual, we can see only visuals. That's why they re-read and wrongly understand that they are doing revision.

For example, when we watch movie for the first time it will be called vision of the movie.

And when we watch the same movie for second time on TV or theater, it will be rightly called RE-VISION of the movie.

Importantly, watching movie again is also equally interesting g that's why we usually watch the movies again and again on TV even if it is already watched by us. But reading the same book or study content looks boring, right! Which means our brain likes RE-VISION but doesn't like re-read.

For making revisions you just need to convert the study content in visual format with the help of brain science methods, what you have already learnt in this book. Than at the time of revision you just need to see the converted images not the text content. That is much easier, faster and interesting.

SO Make VISION before doing RE-VISION.
Let us make intelligent India
All the best.

THANK YOU HAPPY LEARNING

www.ingramcontent.com/pod-product-compliance
Ingram Content Group UK Ltd.
Pitfield, Milton Keynes, MK11 3LW, UK
UKHW041843200726
13854UKWH00005BA/2033

9 789356 113237